Prestige, Privilege and Murder

A Stacie Maroni Mystery

CHRISTA NARDI

Copyright © 2017 Christa Nardi
All rights reserved.

ISBN10 1981720170

Cover design by Victorine Lieske

This is a work of fiction. Although some of the locations may be real, others, like Cold Creek are fictitious. None of these events actually occurred. All characters are the product of the author's imagination. Any resemblance to real people is entirely coincidental.

Other books by Christa Nardi:

The Cold Creek Series by Christa Nardi:
Murder at Cold Creek College (Cold Creek #1)
　Murder in the Arboretum (Cold Creek #2)
　Murder at the Grill (Cold Creek #3)
　Murder in the Theater (Cold Creek #4)
　Murder and a Wedding (Cold Creek #5)

The Hannah and Tamar Mysteries for Young Adults with Cassidy Salem:
　The Mysterious Package (A Hannah and Tamar Mystery)
　Mrs. Tedesco's Missing Cookbook (A Hannah and Tamar Mystery)
　The Misplaced Dog (A Hannah and Tamar Mystery)

CHAPTER 1

It had been a while since I'd gone to a bar by myself and I was nervous. It was a Friday night and the DJ joked about song titles and singles. Not too crowded, a few couples danced to the tune he played. Other couples and groups sat in booths or tables. The bar was long and I'd grabbed the last seat at the bar, a great vantage point for checking out the crowd.

Perched on a stool by the bar, I was on my second glass of wine when I spotted him. A dark-haired Adonis in snug jeans and a tapered polo shirt, he scanned the room. The wine did its job and I felt good. I caught his eye. My soon-to-be ex wasn't the only one who could fool around. I winked and he smiled – his smile about knocked me over. My heart raced as he sauntered in my direction.

"Hi. Care to dance?" He extended his hand and I nodded. The DJ played a slow song and he was a strong lead. I couldn't help but notice the woodsy scent of his aftershave as he held me in his arms and we danced. When the song was over, he walked me back to my spot at the bar.

"Can I buy you a drink?"

"Uh, sure. Viognier, please."

I almost admitted that two was my limit but decided I could sip this one. Viognier isn't the most popular of wines. That he didn't question my choice surprised me. Ted certainly did. Often.

He signaled the bartender and ordered the wine along with a scotch and water for himself. "I'm Rick. Rick Murdock."

I hesitated and answered with a smile, "You can call me Barbie." If this was my once in my lifetime one-night-stand, I didn't want to use my real name.

His eyes narrowed for a split-second before he nodded. The bartender delivered our drinks and distracted him from the name issue.

"Thanks!" I lifted my glass and he tapped it with his.

"Cheers! So, Barbie... what do you think of the music the DJ is serving us?"

I had to give him credit. It was better than the "Come here often?" I expected. Then again, Creekview Lounge catered to a different crowd than Rockies. We exchanged opinions on music and danced to a few more songs.

Along the way, I finished the third glass of wine, gained a better appreciation of the muscles in his shoulders and noticed his hazel eyes. As I tried not to stumble, he caught me.

"You all right?"

I licked my lip, flicked my hair over my shoulder, and tried for a flirty look. "I think some fresh air would help."

His multi-watt smile came back at me and we walked outside. In the parking lot, we commented on how good the crisp cool air felt. He leaned toward me and I toward him. The wine had diminished my inhibitions and I responded when he kissed me. Then his hand was on my back and I burst into tears.

"I'm sorry. I'm so sorry. I just… I can't do this. I'm not as slimy as Ted. I'm so sorry."

He dropped his hands and put them up in front of his body as he stepped back. The smile was long gone. "No problem. No problem."

I turned and ran to my car, still crying. After a few minutes and a little calmer, I drove to my empty townhouse. Thankfully, I didn't get stopped by a police car or have an accident.

It wasn't that late – a little after midnight. That's what I told myself as I called my best friend Jillian. I didn't get any farther than "I hope it's not too late" and I burst into tears.

"Stacie, what's wrong?"

I was crying too hard to talk. I squeaked out, "I went to the Creekview Lounge. I thought I could be like Ted. That's not me. I tried and I can't do this dating thing again."

"Stacie, you are only 34 years old. You have a great job at Foster's Insurance Group. You're educated and smart. Maybe you could go back to school and get that graduate degree in counseling you wanted before Ted."

"I don't know about graduate school. What about all the weight I've gained? I'm not a size 6 anymore. Each day I find another gray hair. The thoughts of going out and trying to meet somebody is scary and tonight proved it."

"You have beautiful dark brown hair and blue eyes, and so what if you're a size 10 now. There's a man out there – a better man than Ted. Did you see any prospects at Creekview?"

"Yeah, there was one guy. His name was Rick. He was a great dancer and when he smiled – wow!"

"So what happened?"

"Well, I said I needed a breath of air and then he kissed me. I just lost it. I mean I'm not even divorced yet. I burst into tears and sat in my car until I could drive. Then I came home and called you because you're my friend." I burst into tears again.

"Stacie, you know if this guy was even halfway good-looking and interested, there's hope. Was he attractive?"

"Oh, he was easy on the eyes for sure. Tall, dark, and handsome. Muscular. And that's not the alcohol talking. I only had a couple glasses of wine."

"Was he drunk?"

"No, he didn't seem drunk at all. He seemed like a nice guy and a good dancer. He wasn't pushy at all and didn't get mad when I freaked. Maybe because I met Ted there ... that was 12 years ago. We were supposed to have a happily ever after."

"Listen, Ted's scum. You have a lot of years left for happiness. Look at me. I didn't meet Wade until I was 30. My thirtieth birthday bash with you and Trina. Remember what fun we had that night?"

We talked more about the fun times. Jillian and I shared some laughs and by the time I hung up I felt much better. I surveyed my townhouse. It had been six months since I bought it and moved in, but it didn't quite feel like home. The only pictures were of my parents and brother, and then a couple of friends. Ted insisted on keeping our dog, Jasper, and I missed him. Maybe I'd get a dog or a cat to keep me company.

The next week, my breakfast on the table, the doorbell rang. When I opened the door, the sight confused me.

"Ma'am. Mrs. Noth?"

"How did you find me?" I asked Rick Murdock as he stood on my front step. Even two weeks later, I hadn't forgotten how good he looked or how humiliated I felt about that night.

"Ma'am. Your address was on the divorce papers. Can we come in please?"

My brain kicked in and I realized Rick wasn't talking – it was the other man on the step. The balding stocky one in uniform with a scowl on his face, a smoker from the odor wafting off of him. And then I realized Rick was in uniform, too. He still looked good with the woodsy scent.

"What's going on?" My gaze went from one man to the other.

"Mrs. Noth, if you don't want us to come in, we can go down to the station. We have some questions we need to ask you."

I stepped aside so they could come inside. "I don't understand. What kind of questions?"

My thoughts were running in circles. Could I have broken a law at the Creekview Lounge that night and not have remembered? Did Rick think I was soliciting? Did they catch me on camera drinking and driving?

"May we sit down? I'm Officer Flatt and this is Officer Murdock."

"Sure… What's going on?"

"Mrs. Noth when was the last time you talked to or saw your husband?"

"As I'm sure he told you, it was yesterday at a meeting with our lawyers. Is he still complaining I refused the 'irreconcilable differences' lies?" My anger at Ted surfaced once again.

"What time was that ma'am?"

"The meeting was at 3:30. I had to leave work early to make it there on time. He finally grabbed the papers and left, must have been after 4. I was home before the 5 o'clock news. I don't understand. Is he accusing me of something? Are you here to serve me a gag order?" I huffed, my anger rising.

I glanced from one officer to the other. Rick avoided my gaze and shuffled his feet.

"No ma'am. Mr. Noth isn't accusing you of anything. He's dead and…"

I didn't hear the rest of his sentence. "What? No!" And then I passed out.

I groaned and opened my eyes. Rick stood there with a glass of water. "Here, drink this."

I sat up and looked to Officer Flatt. "I'm sorry. I don't usually faint. Did you say Ted was dead? That can't be. I just talked to him yesterday."

"That is what I said. He was murdered sometime last night."

"Murdered?"

"Ma'am. After you left your husband yesterday, what did you do?"

"I came home."

"Can anyone vouch for that? Anyone here with you?"

"Huh? What? No one was here with me. It was just me and a half gallon of Rocky Road ice cream." Then it dawned on me. This man suspected I'd killed Ted!

"Oh, my gosh. You think I killed him? I can't even kill spiders."

Officer Flatt shook his head a bit before he answered. "Calm down. We have to ask these questions."

"I'll get you more water." Rick picked up my glass and disappeared into my kitchen. He came back with the water and nodded to Officer Flatt. "One empty Rocky Road carton in the trash."

I glared at him. How dare he check my trash? "Just so you know, I didn't eat it all at once."

His mouth twitched, but he didn't say a word.

"Just a few more questions. About your divorce…"

"Excuse me, but do I need to call my lawyer? I don't think I should talk to you until I call my lawyer.

Of course, he's a divorce attorney, but he must know something about other kinds of law, right?"

Rick was back to staring at the ceiling and Officer Flatt studied the floor. Standing up, Officer Flatt put his little book and pen in his pocket. "We'll be in touch or Detective O'Hare will be if there are any other questions. Here's my card."

He started to leave, Rick following his lead.

"Wait. Has anyone else been notified? Do I need to call his family? What should I tell them? Where is he? Who will take care of the funeral?"

Officer Flatt blinked before he answered. "You'll have to talk with Detective O'Hare at the Beckman Springs Police Department." He shook his head as he turned and left. Rick hesitated and then was gone.

My eggs were cold, but it didn't matter. I'd lost my appetite.

CHAPTER 2

I sat on the sofa, my head in my hands for I don't know how long. I still held the business card and reached for the phone. Time to call this Detective O'Hare and then Jillian. A whole list of people to call came to mind.

"Beckman Springs Police Department, is this an emergency?"

"No, ma'am. Can I speak with Detective O'Hare, please? Officer Flatt told me to call him."

"May I ask who's calling?"

"Stacie Noth."

"Hold on while I transfer your call."

There was silence as I waited. No elevator or perky music when you're on hold for the police department.

"Hello, Mrs. Noth? This is Detective O'Hare."

"Hello. My husband… two officers came by. They said he was dead. Murdered. They said … No, Officer Flatt told me to call you. I've been sitting here trying to understand. Are you sure it's Ted? There must be some mistake."

"I'm sorry, Mrs. Noth. There's no mistake."

I gasped and choked back a sob. "What do I do next? About notifying his parents and family? The funeral?"

"Mrs. Noth, I don't have answers to those questions. As next of kin, you're the only one we've notified officially. I do need to meet with you and get some additional information. Can you come into the station today, say around 11 o'clock?"

"I… I guess. I don't understand what happened, Detective. The officers – they didn't tell me very much."

"We can discuss that when you come in, Mrs. Noth. I'll have more information by then. Shall I send Officer Flatt back to get you or can you get here on your own?"

"Yes, I can do that."

The call disconnected. That's about how I felt. Disconnected. I called Jillian, but the call went straight to voicemail. I left a message that I needed to talk to her immediately and asked her to call no matter what time.

Then I called Nathaniel Heinemann, my divorce attorney. Again, straight to voice mail. This time I left a more pointed message. "Ted's dead. Do you know any criminal lawyers? Call me."

What I really wanted to do was climb back into bed and hide under the covers. My stomach growled and my head hurt. Rocky Road is not the best choice for dinner. I tossed the eggs and ate some cereal but didn't taste a thing. Who identified Ted's body? Who killed him? Why? Other than me, who had a motive?

I was dressed for work, but no longer planned on going there. I called and told Rosie, the receptionist, that I had a family emergency and wouldn't be in.

With another two hours before I'd need to leave for the police station, I started to make lists. Sooner or later someone – probably me – was going to have to call Ted's family. Hopefully, they would take charge of the funeral and burial. Maybe they had a plot for him at the family gravesite. In ten years of marriage, somehow those topics had never come up.

The doorbell rang and startled me. I wasn't expecting anyone. Maybe Officer Flatt was back. I opened the door and a stout, middle-aged man in a uniform man stood there.

"Mrs. Noth? I'm the animal control officer for Beckman Springs. We have a dog from your husband's house – male Maltese, neutered. Will you take him? If not, I'll have to take him to the shelter."

"Jasper? Is he okay? Of course I'll take him."

I stepped outside and the officer led the way. I could hear Jasper's whine and teared up. The officer unlocked the cage. As soon as Jasper saw me, he leapt into my arms.

"Oh, Jasper. I'm so glad you're okay."

I turned to the officer. "His leash? Food?"

"Sorry ma'am. The dog was in the backyard. He's registered to you and his license is up to date. The responding officers provided your new address. You'll need to update the address for the county records."

"Okay. I'll take care of that. First thing I need to do is get him food and a leash. Jasper likes his walks."

The officer smiled. After he left, Jasper and I went into my townhouse. He immediately started to explore. As I found a bowl for water, it occurred to me at least one good thing came from this.

Then it hit me. The police might think Jasper was my motive. Aside from his infidelity, custody of Jasper had been a major bone of contention in negotiating the terms for our divorce. I'd given in on that one to move the process along. Heck, if they gave any consideration to the four-bedroom colonial in the high-end of Beckman Springs Ted lived in, my two-bedroom townhouse didn't quite compare. Yikes.

The phone ringing interrupted my mental listing of my possible motives. Caller ID told me it was my attorney.

"Hi, Nate. Thanks for calling me back."

"Stacie, I'm sorry about Ted. What happened? Why do you need a criminal lawyer?"

"The police said he was murdered. I have a meeting with Detective O'Hare at 11. Nate, they think I killed him."

"Calm down, Stacie. The spouse – especially with the divorce pending – is always the first person they consider. Don't take it personally, okay?"

"Okay, but I don't know what to do. Somebody killed him."

"Do you have an alibi?"

"Can an empty container of Rocky Road testify?"

Nate chuckled. "Make phone calls? Neighbor see you hiding the carton? Did you go for a walk to clear your head?"

"I talked to Jillian. She wanted me to go out with her and Wade. If I'd known I'd need an alibi..."

"Okay. Don't worry too much about that right now. I'll see who I can find just in case. Ted and his father are pretty well connected. Ted was expected to make partner in the next few months. I'll have to avoid lawyers who affiliate with Chameux, Opinsky, & Noonan."

"Partner? And he was complaining about alimony?"

"Stacie, you need to harness your anger when you talk to that detective. Only answer his questions. Don't elaborate. Don't give them extra information. If you think you're digging yourself in a hole say 'I think I'll wait to answer any more questions until my lawyer can be here.' Say it for me."

I repeated his statement several times and wrote it down, then came up with a few variations of my own. As we disconnected, Jasper came and snuggled. I added getting dog food and everything else I'd need for Jasper to the growing list of things to do.

CHAPTER 3

The architectural design of the Beckman Springs police station was not inspiring. A new building, signs pointed to the main entrance. I hesitated as I neared the door. If I didn't meet with the detective now, it might look bad. I just needed to remember what Nate said and stay calm. Taking a deep breath, I hoped I didn't have to use the "I think I'll wait until I have an attorney to finish this discussion" response. If I did, I sure hoped Nate was able to find me one.

I walked in and blinked. Why did a police station need a security screening? Maybe that was because the courthouse and police station shared the same entrance. The little white bowls and the gray crates to put my stuff in reminded me of getting on a plane. Maybe I needed a vacation. Ted and I hadn't taken a vacation for three years. He had been working so hard for partner, or at least that's what I'd believed.

"Ma'am?"

"Sorry. Here you go." I dropped my bag in the crate, placed it on the rollers and walked through the scanner. On the other side, I searched the signs for Detective O'Hare's name.

"Ma'am. Your bag."

"Oh. Thanks. I have an appointment with Detective O'Hare. Can you direct me please?"

"Down the hall to left. Check in at the desk."

I took another deep breath, straightened my back, and marched down the hall to the front desk. From the smell, the cleaning crew had done their job. The female officer at the desk looked up as I approached. She didn't smile, only waited for me to speak.

"Detective O'Hare please. I have an appointment for 11 o'clock."

"Your name, ma'am?"

"Stacie Noth." I cringed at being called "ma'am." It made me feel old.

"Have a seat over there. I'll let him know you're here." She pointed to some wooden benches.

For all its functionality, the bench was anything but comfortable. Even the extra ten pounds I'd put on since turning 30 didn't provide enough of a cushion. I worked on the breathing techniques from my yoga class and reminded myself that I hadn't done anything wrong. Making me wait was manipulative. The detective was probably enjoying a donut.

"Mrs. Noth? Detective O'Hare."

The deep voice didn't prepare me for the tall, attractive man extending his hand. He had brown hair that was messy and in need of a cut. I shook his hand and tried to remember he was the enemy when I looked into his gray eyes.

"Come with me, please. I'm sorry for your loss."

He turned and I followed him down the hall. Given the reason for my visit I chastised myself for appreciating the view. He opened the door to a rather barren room – a table and a few chairs and what I guessed were one-way mirrors. I wondered who was watching. One of the chairs had a sports jacket on it and a file in front of it.

"Have a seat please. Can I get you something to drink? Coffee? Water?" His grim expression belied his courtesy and reminded me why I was there.

"No, thank you. I'm fine. I just want to know what happened to Ted."

"If you don't mind I'll be recording this – just in case there are any issues later on."

He stated his full name Detective Michael James O'Hare, the date and time, and my full name including my maiden name, Maroni.

"Mrs. Noth, do you know why you're here today, meeting with me?"

"Yes sir. Two officers came to my home this morning and told me my husband was murdered. Officer Flatt told me to contact you for additional information."

"So you are here voluntarily, correct?"

I nodded and he commented, "Please respond verbally for the recording" and I did so.

He continued, "Do you have any questions?"

"Yes, sir. What happened? Who killed Ted? What am I supposed to do next? Does his family know? What about his funeral?"

The detective's eyes widened and he put his hands up. "Let's back up. Do you have any questions about this interview?"

My mouth dropped and I glanced around the room. "Okay, who's watching us?"

He blinked and his mouth twitched, but he recovered quickly. "There are three officers – one a female – for your protection, of course. Any other questions about the interview?"

It felt like a test only I hadn't read the chapter. "Do I get a copy of that recording – 'just in case there are any issues later' as you suggested?"

This time his mouth definitely twitched and he looked away before he answered. "Your attorney can request a copy. Do you have an attorney?"

"Only my divorce attorney."

"Any other questions?"

"None that I can think of."

"Okay, one more administrative item before we begin. One of the officers who came to your house this morning – Rick Murdock – do you know him?"

"My husband's dead and you're concerned about a glass of wine I had with one of your officers? I didn't even know he was a cop – excuse me – a policeman."

"You hang out at a cop bar and it doesn't occur to you that the man buying you a drink is a cop?"

"What? Since when is Creekview Lounge a cop bar? I mean I haven't been there for probably 10 years. Back then the clientele were generally businessmen. The crowd still screamed professional that night."

"Creekview Lounge? Not The Brick?"

"Yes, sir. And what would it matter? We didn't hook up. I never saw him again until this morning when he showed up on my front step."

"Okay, okay. Officer Murdock didn't mention this until after the visit to your house. He said he didn't know your name or where you lived. Is that correct?"

"Yes, sir, and if the issue is his behavior, he was a gentleman. Can we talk about Ted now?"

He still looked skeptical, his brows knitted and mouth set. He pulled a notepad from his pocket and cleared his throat.

"I'm going to ask you some of the same questions Officer Flatt asked you earlier. I hope you don't mind. When was the last time you saw your husband?"

I exhaled and remembered Nate's warning to only answer the question. "Yesterday at 3:30 pm."

He hesitated, consulted his notes, and asked, "Where was that?"

"At the office of Nathaniel Heinemann."

He dropped his chin and made eye contact, as if to encourage me to continue and I waited.

"Who is that and what was the purpose of this meeting?"

"My divorce attorney. We were discussing the divorce agreement."

He consulted his notes again. "Was there an issue with the agreement, a point of contention?"

"Ted wanted the reference to his adultery removed and replaced with 'irreconcilable differences.' I refused."

"And how did that end?"

"Mr. Heinemann advised him that he could either sign the agreement by 5 pm today or we'd see him in court and he could make his argument to the judge. Ted grabbed the papers and left."

"And what did you expect would happen?"

"We expected he'd have it couriered over to Mr. Heinemann's by 5 pm today."

"Why would he give in and not force the court hearing?"

"He's up . . . " I choked back a sob. "He was up for partner at Chameux, Opinsky & Noonan – CO&N, and a hearing could hurt him more than a single entry in the decree." I opened my mouth to add "Who reads divorce decrees anyways?" But closed my mouth.

Detective O'Hare studied his notes before his next question. "Do you own a gun, Mrs. Noth?"

"He was shot? No, I don't own a gun. Never shot one. Didn't want to. Didn't want one in the house."

"Yes, your husband was shot. Did he own a gun?"

"Not that I know of…"

He cocked his head. All of Nate's advice left my head.

"I didn't know about Meredith either. If he could have a mistress, he could have a gun. Is she the one who found him?"

"Do you know Meredith's full name?"

I glared at him for not answering my question. "Meredith Jones Langford."

At his raised eyebrows, I added, "Yes, Senator Langford's daughter. Now will you tell me who found Ted, who identified him? Maybe they made a mistake."

Several expressions quickly passed across his face, too quick for me to guess what he was thinking.

"Ms. Jerilyn Walters called 9-1-1. She said she heard the dog barking and howling in the backyard sometime after midnight. When she went for a run this morning the dog started barking again and whimpering. She could see the open side door but the storm door was closed."

"She's his neighbor. Did she identify him?"

Detective O'Hare cleared his throat. "She was shown a picture and identified him at the scene. His fingerprints are on file and his identity has been confirmed. I'm sorry."

I started to cry and he left without a word. He returned with a glass of water. I wiped my face with my hands, remembered the tissue in my purse, and wiped off my face. "Thank you."

"I only have a few more questions. Your husband kept the house and you moved out?"

"After I walked in on them one afternoon, I didn't want anything to do with my so-called dream house. I only went back to pack my things and serve the divorce papers in person. We maintained separate accounts. I bought my townhouse with my own money."

"Now won't you inherit the house though?"

"Not unless something changed I don't know about. His father 'gave' us that house as a wedding gift but kept the deed in his name. According to Ted, Mr. Noth didn't want to take the chance I could somehow wiggle out of the prenup. Maybe the real reason was he knew his son better than I did. Otherwise the house would be on the market."

The detective's mouth dropped and he just stared at me. I shrugged. Then he put on the grim game face again.

"Thank you for your assistance in this, Mrs. Noth. Perhaps I can answer your other questions. About the funeral and such you probably should contact Mr. Noth's family or would you prefer I take care of that?"

"I haven't talked to Mr. Noth since the day I moved out six months ago. He came to be sure I wasn't taking anything that belonged to him. If someone else could handle that call I'd appreciate it. If you could let me know once he's been notified, I'll call him, Ted's office, and our friends."

"It's the least we can do under the circumstances."

"Will you keep me informed of the investigation please?"

"Yes ma'am, to the extent that we can. Legally, you are still his wife. Anything else?"

I shook my head. He concluded the interview with the date and the time and turned off the recorder as he rose. He opened the door and waved me forward.

"Ladies room?"

"Down the hall, first door on your right."

I'd reached the door when I heard O'Hare's deep voice.

"Murdock, what were you doing at Creekview Lounge?"

I heard the murmur of laughter and multiple voices, without catching what was said. Then O'Hare spoke again.

"Definitely a different class of women if she's any indication." He walked into the room and the door closed.

CHAPTER 4

I was on the way to my car when Jillian called. I filled her in with an abbreviated version.

"Stacie, I'm so sorry. I mean Ted was scum but I'm sorry you have to deal with this on top of everything else. Let me know what I can do to help. Wade, too."

"Thanks, Jillian."

"I have to run to the manager's meeting. I'll call you when I finally get to eat lunch."

We disconnected and I noticed I'd missed a call. My voicemail had a message from Nate to remind me to call him after the interview. I needed to debrief and he was a good sounding board. His admin put me through with no wait.

"Stacie what happened? How did it go?"

"I did just what you said, Nate. I think it threw the detective off. One thing though – at the beginning he asked me if I had any questions about the interview. Are there questions he expected me to ask? Questions I should have asked."

"I'm not sure I know what you mean. I hope you didn't ask 'am I a suspect?' Or 'do I need an attorney' or something similar."

"No, I didn't ask those. I asked who was watching though. Anyway, Ted was shot. I don't own a gun and I never shot one. He also asked about the house and I explained it really belonged to Ted's father not Ted. I don't think I'm a suspect anymore."

"Stacie, be careful. Don't get too comfortable. What about Ted's will? He had one right?"

"I... I don't know. Nate, we're only in our 30s. We weren't thinking about death. At least I wasn't."

"He was a lawyer, Stacie, and his father and grandfather before him. I bet he had one. I'd be very surprised if he didn't. Depending on what it says you could have a motive."

"I doubt it. If he was efficient enough to write one, don't you think he changed it by now? How many more things about Ted am I going to find out about?"

"We'll see. I did get a name for a criminal attorney if you need one. And one of the other attorneys here specializes in estate law if you need her. What about the funeral?"

"I don't know. The detective is going to notify Ted's father. He'll let me know when that's taken care of and I'll call to express my condolences and find out how he wants to handle it. I doubt Hamilton Noth will let anything not be in his control. Then I'll call Ted's office and mutual friends. Not sure who will tell Meredith. I suspect it will be on the news tonight. In fact, I probably need to call my office and officially notify them I'll be out for the next few days."

"Do that and keep me posted, okay? Use my private number."

"Will do. Thanks for everything, Nate."

I stopped and picked up food, a bed, and toys for Jasper. I dictated a reminder to contact the vet and change the information on his tag and Home Again. There was no telling if Ted had kept up with Jasper's monthly combo pack.

I no sooner got home and my phone rang. It was O'Hare letting me know Ted's father had been notified. I found his name in my contact list. I so hated dealing with the man. If he had been murdered, I'd be a suspect for sure.

"Mr. Noth, please. This is Stacie Noth calling."

"One moment please."

"Hello, Stacie. You've heard I presume."

"Yes, sir. I'm sorry for your loss."

"Thank you, Stacie. Given your estranged status with my son, I was surprised to hear you are no longer a serious suspect."

I took a deep breath and ignored his comment. "I called to express my condolences to the family and to find out how you would like to handle the funeral."

"Aren't you and Ted divorced?"

"He hadn't signed the papers yet, so legally we're still married. Separated but married."

"I see. We will take care of the funeral. I will keep you updated. If you're still married, it wouldn't look right if you weren't present. We must keep up appearances."

He disconnected without even a goodbye or a thank you for calling. Rude as usual and more concerned with appearances than anything else. Once again, I wondered if the man even had a heart. I played with Jasper for a few minutes and got us both settled down.

For the next hour or so I made calls. I called Rosie at the office to make it official, Ted's office, my parents, and then the list of mutual friends. By the third or fourth call, I was on auto-pilot, the same refrain each time.

"I just wanted to let you know before you heard it on the news. Ted was murdered last night… The police are investigating – maybe a burglar who knows? … I don't know the details yet. …Ted's father is taking care of the arrangements… Of course, I'll let you know."

Some asked more questions like whether I would move back to the house or come back to the country club. Not likely as I was never comfortable in either place. Some shared gossip. Apparently Meredith and I had more in common than Ted. If the rumor mill was on target, she walked in on him with the housekeeper. I shuddered at that one and presumed he'd fired the older Mrs. Vittone and hired a younger woman.

While an undergraduate, I did some work at the local battered women's shelter with hopes of getting a graduate degree in counseling. That dream never materialized, nonetheless I did the volunteer training and still helped out at the shelter each week. I wasn't sure how I'd feel by Saturday when I was scheduled to be there. That call would wait. Most weeks I also volunteered at Pet Connections over the weekend, especially once I'd moved out. I'd check in with them next week.

All done, I was exhausted. I cuddled with Jasper and turned on the news just in time. A recent photo of Ted smiling and appearing distinguished appeared on the screen. His blonde hair, blue eyes, tan, and athletic build always brought to mind a California beach boy. He was always so full of life.

Breaking news tonight. A murder in Beckman Springs' most exclusive gated community, River's Edge. Mr. Theodore Jackson Noth was found dead in his home this morning, an apparent victim of foul play. Beckman Springs police are withholding details of the open investigation but ask anyone who has information to please contact them at the number on the screen.

The broadcaster no sooner cut to the traffic problems and the commute from Reston to DC and my phone rang, and rang, and rang. My father, among others, sorry he was too far away to be of help. I assured him all was well. I cut him short as more calls were coming in. People it hadn't occurred to me to call, some of whom I barely knew. The former to see how I was doing; the latter to get any dirt I was willing to share. Amazingly, some of them didn't realize Ted and I were separated.

I thought I was done with the phone and it rang again. My phone showed a Reston area code and number but no name. Although I normally wouldn't answer, given the news announcement, I answered.

"Mrs. Noth? Stacie Noth?"

"Yes, this is she. May I ask who's calling?"

"Of course. This is Mr. Trichter, your husband's attorney. First, allow me to express my condolences."

"Thank you." I didn't understand so I waited for him to explain.

"Mr. Hamilton Noth contacted me regarding Ted's demise. You're named in Ted's will. There will be a reading of the will, tomorrow at 3 pm at Mr. Hamilton Noth's home. Your presence is requested."

"Thank you, Mr. Trichter. I'll be there."

I hung up and immediately called Jillian. If she could come with me, I wouldn't be alone. There'd be at least one friendly face in the room.

Jillian answered and launched into an apology. "Work was nuts and Reinhardt was at her witchiest. I finally got back to my desk about the time you called Rosie with the news. Trina and I decided to order in. Everyone is worried about you, of course. Even Reinhardt was disturbed by the idea of a murderer in Beckman Springs. How are you doing, Stacie?"

"Okay. I keep expecting to wake up and discover this is a bad dream and feel guilty for dreaming Ted was dead. Then the doorbell or the phone rings. It's real and Ted's dead."

"Who's taking care of the funeral?"

"Ted's father, of course. And I should be there for the sake of appearances. Like I wouldn't go to the funeral to pay my respects. It will be so awkward though."

"I can take time off and go with you when you find out when. You shouldn't have to be alone with the Noth family and entourage."

"Thanks, Jillian. Any chance you could take off tomorrow, too? Ted's attorney just called and I've been told to attend the reading of the will."

"Ted had a will? Did you know?"

"Yes, apparently he did. Another thing I didn't know about. Can you come with me?"

"I can do one or the other. I took time off for my mother. You pick one, okay? Maybe Trina or Nate for the other?" Of the three of us friends, Trina tended to walk on the wild side. That would not go over well on the Noth estate.

"Funeral then. I'll see if Nate can come with me tomorrow. He'd at least follow all the legalese."

Jillian brought me up to date with good news on her mother's breast cancer and some of the gossip at work.

After I hung up, I called Nate's private number and left a message. Nate called back and agreed to accompany me. He also suggested, although it might be risky, that I notify O'Hare of the reading.

"Noth is rushing the reading of the will. What's the rush? That to me is a red flag. The detective might find it curious as well."

"What would be the down side to my letting him know?"

"The biggest risk is that the will could give you a motive. If somehow the house had been deeded to

Ted, for example. Too bad you don't know what it says."

"Nate, I don't think that happened. And wouldn't he find out about it sooner or later anyway?"

"Your call, Stacie. I'll see you at the Noth mansion tomorrow afternoon."

I considered the options and figured it was best to be open. I didn't expect to be the recipient of much from the estate, if anything. I placed the call before I could chicken out.

"Detective O'Hare, please. This is Stacie Noth."

"One moment, please."

"Mrs. Noth, Detective O'Hare. What can I do for you?" He sounded gruff. I glanced at the clock and realized he must work 12-hour shifts.

"I wanted to let you know about the reading of the will. Mr. Trichter called at Mr. Noth's request and told me it will be tomorrow at 3 pm at Mr. Noth's home – Mr. Hamilton Noth's home, not Ted's obviously."

"That was fast. Thanks for letting me know." He disconnected without another word.

It was 6:30 and if I rushed I could make it to the 7 pm yoga class. With the extra stress, it was time for some self-care before moving on to the next problem.

CHAPTER 5

Nate stood at the top of the circular driveway. As always, he wore a gray suit, his white hair perfectly coiffed, his blue eyes bright. Nate was the closest to family I had in Virginia. In his sixties, he had been a family friend as far back as I could remember. Over the past several months, as I dealt with the divorce, he'd been like a father to me.

"About time. You look good in black."

I glanced down in at my one black sheath. Not designer quality, but acceptable.

"Thanks. It's all I had."

"I don't know all the people who already arrived. An older woman with a cane, a couple about your age, and two men. One with a tailored suit that puts my wardrobe to shame."

"The older woman? Very petite and thin?"

He nodded.

"That would be Mrs. Vittone, our housekeeper. The couple is probably Ted's sister Maureen and her husband. Shall we go in and find out who the others are?"

He smiled and took my arm. The door opened before we had a chance to knock. A nondescript woman waved us in and escorted us to the main living area without saying more than "this way." Then she disappeared. Exquisitely furnished and appointed, the room was without warmth – extravagant, yet austere.

Hamilton Noth was in his usual polo shirt and khaki pants. His shirt was fitted enough to show off how often he worked out. He conversed with a man who matched Nate's description of the well-suited man at one end of the polished wooden bar. Shorter than Mr. Noth, the man looked to be about my age, fair haired and fair skinned with glasses. Mr. Noth did all the talking, while the other man listened intently.

Another man stood at the other end. I recognized him as Maureen's husband. He wore dress pants and shirt, buttons bulging, and hair thinning. Stubble dotted his chin; he needed a shave. He nursed a beer and watched everyone.

Standing off to the side, as if to fade into the background, was the detective. He wore the same sports jacket I'd seen before. He nodded when we made eye contact and then glanced to others in the room. I realized he and I were the only ones in the room who weren't blonde.

"Okay, Stacie. Who is who?" Nate whispered.

"The man over there is Detective O'Hare. Son-in-law is drinking at the bar. Maureen and Ted's mom, Isabel, are the two on the sofa. Mrs. Vittone is the older woman in the wingback chair. My guess is the well-dressed man Mr. Noth is talking to is Mr. Trichter."

"Anyone else coming?"

"Not that I know of. His paternal grandparents live in California somewhere. I doubt they've gotten here yet. No one ever talks about Isabel's side of the family. I always got the sense that the male line was the only family important to them. Mr. Noth only talked about the importance of Ted having a son."

The woman who had let us in wheeled in a cart and set an array of food on the bar. She poured coffee and then disappeared again. Nate raised his eyebrows like I would know what was up with the food. I shrugged. Mr. Noth waved to the food with a "Help yourself." No one did.

Mr. Noth joined his wife and daughter on the sofa. He dwarfed both of the women as they huddled together. The attorney moved to the vacant wingback chair and cleared his throat.

"Good afternoon. Shall we get started? I'm Mr. Cyrus Trichter, Ted's attorney and the executor of his will." His voice was nasal and he spoke slowly. He cleared this throat again.

"Mr. Noth and I agreed to skip the standard verbiage and get to the bequests. First, though, please keep in mind that exact values, unless specifically stated, will not be known until the estate is fully settled." He stopped and paused to confirm he had everyone's undivided attention.

"Ted wrote this part himself, in the first person. His wish was that I read it as written." He cleared his throat again and read, "I bequeath the bulk of my estate to my father, Mr. Hamilton Jefferson Noth, who provided me with the means to rise to my current position in life. He made me who I am and is ultimately responsible not only for my successes, but my failures. He was always quick to give me what was needed for appearance sake."

Mr. Noth hissed and Maureen jumped at the honesty and bitterness of Ted's words. It occurred to me that his father's push and attitude likely somehow contributed to Ted's death as well.

"To my younger sister, Maureen Noth Dantzig…" He paused and all eyes turned to her. "Who had the misfortune of being a woman and didn't receive the same support from our father, I bequeath a $500,000 trust fund to enable her to pursue her career choice and not be dependent on her husband for her identity or her life."

Amidst a few gasps, Mr. Trichter shuffled papers and then explained, "There are lots of rules on how Maureen can access these funds 'unless of course she divorces her husband, who despite Maureen's denials I believe is responsible for her multiple injuries over the years. After all, as a gymnast she didn't have as many bruises or broken bones as she's had in the past few years.' Those were Mr. Ted Noth's words."

Mr. Trichter paused again. He turned to Maureen. "In this envelope are photos he gave to me to be given to you in the presence of witnesses."

Maureen was petite and her body shook as she sobbed. Her head was down and Mr. Trichter placed the envelope on her lap.

As I glanced over to her husband, Mitch, he slithered out the door. O'Hare was right behind him. They both returned with the detective between Mitch and the door.

Mr. Trichter cleared his throat. "Shall we go on?"

Mr. Noth nodded, clearly not happy with what he'd heard. He didn't look surprised though. I knew Ted had shared his suspicions with his father. Mr. Noth had discounted his concerns. After all, Mitch was the son of one the senior partners in Noth, Jenkins, and Dantzig and owner of one of the largest real estate management companies on the East coast. I suspected Mr. Noth knew it was coming and for once was powerless to stop the concerns being made public.

"To my wife, Stacie Maroni Noth…"

Now all eyes were on me and Nate patted my arm.

Mr. Trichter continued, "Who tried to retrain me to think of women as equals, who refused to be dependent on me, but always supported me, I bequeath $100,000 to allow her to return to school or otherwise further her career. Also, whatever she wishes of the furnishings of the house we shared, with listed exceptions which revert to my father as they belong to him."

I blinked back tears. A lot, but not enough in the grand scheme of things to provoke murder. Well, unless Hamilton Noth was the victim.

"To Mrs. Doria Vittone, a valued employee, I bequeath the sum of $50,000 to help with her expenses in the future." Everyone turned to her and she nodded. She appeared frailer than I remembered. So thin and bent over.

"Finally, I bequeath $10,000 each to Pet Connections and Cornerstone Community Women's Shelter." He paused. "That completes Mr. Noth's last will and testament. It will be filed tomorrow with the Circuit Court, and anyone wishing to read it can get copies. Any parties wishing to contest any aspect of this will and testament can do so. The first and hopefully final accounting will be completed within the next four months and submitted to the Commissioner of Accounts, who will oversee and ensure the estate is handled properly. At that time, probate tax must be paid by the estate prior to any distribution. Said will be done from his accounts prior to any distribution. As his wife, the responsibility for filing the last income tax return will rest with Mrs. Noth. I will be available to help in any way when the time comes as Ted would have wished."

Nate patted my arm again. "I'll email you the contact information for the estate attorney I mentioned. We'll deal with it when the time comes."

No one said anything for a few minutes. Mr. Trichter turned to Mr. Noth. "Hamilton, are you going to share the funeral arrangements?"

"Yes, of course. We have been informed that we will be able to hold the funeral on Thursday. We will gather at the Cunningham Funeral Home at 10 o'clock to celebrate Ted's life with burial at 11:30 at Celestial Gardens Cemetery in the family sector. Per Ted's request, he will be cremated. There will be no additional visitation hours. Thank you for coming today."

His presentation was devoid of emotion and dismissive. As I stood to leave, he moved into my path and took hold of my arm. "Mr. Trichter will meet you at the house…" He looked at his watch and continued, "in one hour to remove whatever you wish if that is acceptable."

We both knew that was not a question but an order. Better to get it over with than to disagree. On a whim I walked over to O'Hare. "Mr. Trichter is meeting me at Ted's house in an hour. Is that okay?"

He glanced at his watch and then from Mitch to Maureen. He nodded.

I walked over to Maureen and squeezed her shoulders. "I'm so sorry. If there's anything I can do…"

She gave no response, her eyes red and swollen. Ted and I had offered support before on multiple occasions so I didn't expect anything else.

Outside, Nate gave me a quick hug. "Stacie, to most that's a good-sized inheritance; however, the alimony wasn't exactly small change. Besides, you have your own accounts that are not part of his estate."

"So I'm in the clear, right?"

He chuckled. "If I were a betting man, I'd say yes. Even so, be careful, Stacie. You're not off the hook until they find the person who killed him. You'll also have to file the income tax for each of you. We'll deal with that when the time comes."

More than a little overwhelmed, I nodded.

"You know, he wasn't a bad man. He tried so hard to get Maureen to admit what was happening. We both did. It will be hard to deny now, even for Hamilton Noth."

"Is there anyway the police could turn his donations to either of those charities to look bad for you?"

"Huh? I do volunteer at both those places, but I have nothing to do with the management or finances of either. Ted and his father supported those activities. Volunteering was something Ted's wife was expected to do. And those were a few things I was expected to do that I actually enjoyed. Ted came out to Pet Connections a few times to help out as well. It's where we found Jasper. He routinely stopped at Cornerstone to provide free legal counseling and referrals. I'm a little surprised though he didn't include Jasper in his will."

"Do you think he doubted whether you would take Jasper, Stacie? I've dealt with divorces where child custody was less emotional than you two were about Jasper. Do you need me to come to the house with you?"

"No need. I appreciate your coming with me today. I'll keep you posted if anything else happens or if I need either of the two attorneys you mentioned."

He gave me another hug and we both left.

CHAPTER 6

I pulled into Starbucks for coffee and called Jillian. She didn't pick up so I left a voicemail "Will read. Funeral is Thursday morning. Call me when you can."

At River's Edge, I pulled up to the guard house and electric gate. The guard's greeting was polite enough, though it was lacking the friendliness he'd shown when I lived there. His gray uniform and scowl added to my misgivings.

"Hello, Mrs. Noth. We haven't seen you in some time. Sorry about Mr. Noth. The senior Mr. Noth called and said you were to go to the house."

The gate opened and my car drove on autopilot around the fountain in the center green space across from the entrance. I parked in front of the house and waited. When a cruiser pulled up, I got out of my car. Officer Flatt and a female officer joined me. Her nametag read "Napoli." I wondered what part of Italy her family came from, but didn't ask.

Flatt waved his arm toward the house. "Detective O'Hare said to meet you here. Shall we?"

"This is as far as I'm going until Mr. Trichter arrives. I don't have a key or the code for the door for one thing. I also don't want to be accused of stealing anything on the 'don't take' list."

The officers looked confused so I introduced myself to Officer Napoli and explained the purpose of the visit. A few minutes later, Mr. Trichter arrived.

"Mrs. Noth?" He asked as he gaped at the officers. From his stiff jaw, raised brows, and rigid posture, I could tell he wasn't any more happy to be there than I was.

"This is an open investigation and a crime scene, Mr.?" Officer Flatt answered Trichter's unasked question with his own.

"Trichter. I see. Let's get this over with then."

He exhaled and took a step forward, leading the rest of us to the front door. As he went to enter the code, the door opened.

"Officers, Mr. Noth will be very disturbed to find that the door was left ajar and not locked. Obviously, you didn't set the alarm either. You will hear from him."

He took a few steps inside and turned around, his eyes wide. "What kind of animals are you? What have you done?"

Napoli slipped past the red-faced attorney while Flatt stood speechless. "Flatt, this room at least has been trashed. Better call O'Hare."

Flatt glared at me. "Not me. Check with the guard at the gate house. He clocks everyone in and I wasn't here much more than a minute before you. Besides, I don't have a key or the code."

Flatt signaled for Napoli to watch us. She nodded and he jumped in the car and took off. Napoli moved her arms to get us out of the doorway. "Over here folks. We'll wait for Detective O'Hare."

Mr. Trichter made an exaggerated show of peering at his watch and huffed. "This was supposed to take only 30 minutes. I have an appointment at 5. Mrs. Noth and I will have to reschedule."

He made like he was going to leave, except Officer Napoli moved in front of him. She was petite but her stance communicated her intent to stop him if he tried to get past her. "Sorry, sir, no one leaves without Detective O'Hare's say-so."

Mr. Trichter stomped his feet, his face getting red. He entertained us with lots of profanity. An adult tantrum if I ever saw one. He stomped down the sidewalk and pulled out his phone.

Flatt returned and got out of the car. "He clocked her in two minutes before us. O'Hare is on his way. I'm gonna check the house."

He reappeared a few minutes later shaking his head. "The whole house looks like this front room. I was the responding and, other than the office where we found him, everything was pristine at that time."

Napoli nodded and I shrugged. My phone played Jillian's ring tone as O'Hare pulled up. I let her call go to voicemail. "Flatt, Napoli, Mrs. Noth."

He glanced over toward Mr. Trichter and raised his eyebrows.

"He's mad we wouldn't let him leave until you got here." Napoli smirked as she spoke.

Mr. Trichter became more agitated.

O'Hare exhaled. "He's going to be even less happy, but I'm guessing Mr. Noth is giving him his orders now."

Sure enough, Mr. Trichter was having another tantrum, stomping his feet, one arm flailing, the other holding his phone. I half expected him to fling the thing.

"Mrs. Noth, it's up to you. Mr. Noth suggested that you would know if anything was missing better than he, other than what's on the list. Mr. Trichter has the list. What do you say?" He peered at me with his big gray eyes and waited for my response. I just wanted to get this over with.

"Okay, on one condition. Can I get Jasper's toys and stuff? That's all I want out of the house anyway."

"That shouldn't be a problem." O'Hare turned to Flatt. "Collect Mr. Trichter and let's get this over with. Napoli, you stay here with them, while we…" He pointed to himself and the two other officers who had joined the party before he continued, "check out the house and get pictures. I'll signal you when Mrs. Noth and Mr. Trichter can come in."

And we waited. I wasn't sure what to expect. When we walked in I gasped at the mess. Cushions on the floor, side tables turned over, books all over the floor, paintings askew. I bent over to pick up a book – a first edition no less – and O'Hare pulled my arm back.

"Don't touch anything folks, especially anything that might have fingerprints. Just tell us if anything is missing." He dropped his voice and leaned toward me. "And no bending over in that dress please – it's distracting."

My mouth dropped as I turned to him and he chuckled. I looked down at my basic black sheath. It wasn't all that short. Then again it might be shorter than I thought. Mr. Trichter stood in the room and scanned his list. He shook his head and mumbled something I didn't catch.

"What did you say Mr. Trichter? Is there a problem?" O'Hare demanded.

"I don't know. I don't know. This list isn't by room. It's in alphabetical order for pity sake. Ted told me his father was difficult, but this is insane."

Controlling my desire to laugh, I decided to speed the process up. "The paintings on the walls are the same ones that were there when I moved out. Other than crooked, they haven't been touched. Ted's mother's China pieces are scattered. Dresden if that helps, Mr. Trichter. I can't tell if any are missing. I never counted them. At least whoever did this didn't break them."

"There were several special edition and first edition books like this one." I pointed at the one on the floor. "I'm not sure if they're on the list or not. I never knew if they were Ted's or his father's. One is an Andy Warhol, another by Norman Rockwell. There was one from the 1800s on wealth, Hemingway, Faulkner, and others. I don't know all the names."

Mr. Trichter smiled. "Got the China, Rockwell and Warhol. I see some other books on here too. Got the paintings. Thankfully, they are all signed. Mostly the list is of paintings, books, china, silver, and some electronics. Oh, and an Althorp antique desk." He walked around the room, shaking his head and marking his list.

"The desk is in Ted's study or it was. China and silver are mostly in the dining room, though there are crystal figurines and China plates for decoration in the main living room and occasionally in other rooms. Electronics will be in the game room down the hall, his office, and the master bedroom unless he moved them."

O'Hare asked, "Why all the electronics? Sounds a bit excessive."

"Ted liked his toys – video games of all types. Often, if we had friends over the men would all end up in the game room. There's also a pool table in there. In his office, he had a secured set up for work. Part of what he did for a while involved technology-related issues and he used a separate computer to sign into the CO&N server with better firewalls. He dealt with issues of copyright and infringement of copyright, including of computer games. I don't know if he was still doing any of that."

"We're done downstairs. We'll be upstairs," the officer with the camera interjected and took the steps two at a time. His partner followed him.

O'Hare nodded and moved through each room with the same mess. I helped Mr. Trichter check off what was obvious. Clearly whoever did this was not into art or books. Until I'd seen how much the paintings and books were appraised for by the insurance company, I hadn't realized their value. Professional burglars would have taken the paintings for sure.

CHAPTER 7

I stumbled when I walked into Ted's office or what was left of it. It was the metallic odor and the dark stains on his desk and floor that got to me.

"Mrs. Noth, are you alright?" Flatt barked from the other side of the room.

I tried to nod and next thing I knew O'Hare was holding me up. He walked me to the stairs.

"Sit down on the step and put your head down, take a few deep breaths. Don't move." He turned and yelled, "Napoli, come over here and stay with Mrs. Noth."

He disappeared and came back with a cold bottle of water and placed it behind my neck. After a few minutes, he handed it to me. I raised my eyebrows at the bottle but took it. From Napoli's similar expression, she also waited for an explanation.

"I figured he wouldn't miss it and I'm pretty sure it's not on Mr. Trichter's list. Feel better? Did you notice anything?"

"Other than the smell and blood? They didn't like art but the second computer is gone. CO&N will know if it should be there. His computer and screens – why did they destroy them? Look for an external hard drive. He backed everything up each night. He was OCD about that."

He made notes and left me on the steps. I heard him direct Flatt to search for the hard drive. Napoli stayed with me. "Is there a safe he should be looking for?"

"I wasn't allowed in Ted's office, so I don't know. If there is, I don't know who would have the combination."

Married to the man for ten years, I was only now aware of all I didn't know. Mr. Trichter wandered past us and nodded. Napoli stepped away from me and I heard her talking to someone, but couldn't hear what she said. She and O'Hare came over to me after a few minutes.

"Safe is behind the painting of the southern plantation. Any idea where he might have written down the combination? His preferred combinations?"

"When we traveled and used a safe in the hotel, he always used 3232. That's how old his father was when he made partner and how old Ted expected to be when he made partner – he didn't make that goal though."

"Any idea why not? Were there issues at work?"

"No. Not that I know of. I think over the years the level of work equity required increased. Winning clients over and keeping them took more effort and time."

"Okay." He looked up at the stairs. "Cameron! You guys almost done up there?"

"Just finished, sir." The officer with the camera loped down the stairs past me.

"I need you in here while I see if we can open the safe."

They disappeared from my sight. I heard O'Hare curse, then he came back to the stairs. "Any other suggestions?"

"Afraid not. For the past three years, since he turned 32, we haven't gone on a vacation. He was driven – no pushed – to do whatever it took to make partner. He worked late, at least that's what he always told me. For sure, I know he spent hours in his office when he was home. Sorry."

"You told Napoli you weren't allowed in his study?"

"That's correct. He said all the papers in there were confidential, proprietary. When he wasn't in the office, it was locked. Even Mrs. Vittone couldn't go in there. He vacuumed in there, emptied whatever trash there was, and added the shredded papers to the recycling." As I said it out loud, I realized how odd that sounded.

O'Hare shook his head. "Okay, we'll have to get someone over here to get into the safe. We found the dog bed for you. In the meantime, let's finish up with Mr. Trichter's list."

O'Hare put aside Jasper's bed, leash, and his favorite dinosaur toys. We continued with the downstairs. The game room was a mess, all the electronics and books scattered, the large screen twisted. The pool table upended. Mr. Trichter checked off the paintings. Upstairs was much of the same. Drawers turned upside down, belongings scattered or destroyed. If they'd stolen anything, it wasn't obvious. It also wasn't obvious what they'd been searching for.

"My first reaction was that a gang realized the house was empty when the murder was in the news. Figured the house was prime to steal high class merchandise. Now it seems like whoever it was, they were looking for something and got mad when they couldn't find it. Any ideas?" O'Hare turned to me, eyebrows raised.

I shook my head. "If they were after 'high class' merchandise, they didn't recognize it when they found it. No idea what he was working on. Mr. Chameux, the senior partner, might have an idea, or Mr. Opinsky."

It was late and I was tired when O'Hare finally let Mr. Trichter and me leave. I called Jillian as I drove out of River's Edge. She invited me over so she could hear about everything and not have to repeat it all to Wade. It was on my way home and I needed the support.

Jillian and Wade both met me at the door with a three-way hug. My mouth watered at the sight of the snack food and cheese they had set out and I realized I was starving. Chinese delivery was the main meal. In between bites, I related the afternoon's activities. I might have exaggerated Trichter's tantrums as we enjoyed the Chinese takeout. Each part of the story included another police officer and I couldn't help but mention how good looking both Rick and the detective were.

"Now don't go dragging Jillian to a cop bar. And certainly not Trina. The trouble you three could get into," Wade teased. He shook his head.

"Not sure they're exactly impressed with me. I keep fainting, I'm a suspect, and I may have given the detective a show besides. So embarrassing."

"What kind of a show, Stacie? What did you do?" Jillian's eyes were wide and her voice had an edge to it.

"It wasn't on purpose. I bent over to pick up a book up off the floor – it was a first edition. The detective made some crack about not bending over in this dress so I don't know if he got a show or not. He said it was distracting." I shrugged, an effort to make light of it.

Jillian laughed and Wade shook his head. "How can we tell unless you bend over?"

I turned around and told myself it was an experiment and bent over as if to reach for something. Then I turned around. Now Jillian was shaking her head and trying not to laugh.

Wade chuckled. "I almost want to tell you the color of your panties and make you think he saw them. Close though, and he's right about distracting."

"Then how could you tell me the color?" I asked, not sure if I could believe him.

"Stacie, one of the things I know about you – just from listening to you and Jillian mind you – is that everything has to match. You're wearing a black dress and black shoes, so you are probably wearing black undies and a black bra. Am I right?"

As much as I wanted to say no, he was right. "There's nothing wrong with having things match, you know."

The both laughed, their laughter interrupted by the standard ring tone of my phone. I normally hated to answer an unknown caller or take a call when visiting friends, but given the circumstances, I did.

"Hello, who is this, please?"

"Detective O'Hare. Mrs. Noth I have a few questions if you have a few minutes."

"What kind of questions, Detective." I glanced at Jillian and Wade. Both of them leaned toward me, not laughing any more.

"What can you tell me about the security at River's Edge?"

"It's a gated community. Only people the security guard recognizes or who have been cleared by a resident can gain access during the day. Unless things changed, the guard is on duty from 7 am to 9 pm. When there's no guard, the only way in is with a code and using the code activates the surveillance cameras. Does that help?"

"How often are codes changed?"

"Whenever there is a need, I guess. The codes are resident driven. Ted's father had the code changed when I moved out."

"I'm trying to figure out how someone got into River's Edge. Any ideas?"

"Detective, the obvious possibilities would be that the person's name was left with the guard, the person had the code, or they climbed over the fence. There are surveillance cameras and they're not only triggered by the code, but by movement. That's how they figured out who burglarized some of the houses a while back. Ted didn't want to pay the extra for motion activated cameras around the house but the management company should have the other footage."

"Any idea who Ted would have given the code to?"

"Mrs. Vittone and then the new housekeeper. Though I assume she'd only come during the day and wouldn't need the gate code. They'd need the house code though and the alarm code. He may have changed it again after Mrs. Vittone left. His father always had the code for the gate, the house, and the alarm system. I don't know who else." I wasn't sure if he would have given the code to Meredith. Maybe. How else could she have surprised him?

"Your husband was found in his study with the door open. I have a note here that he locked himself in his study when he worked at home. That would seem to mean whoever it was had to first gain access to River's Edge, then the house, and then the office."

"Detective, when I lived there and was home, or when Mrs. Vittone was there cleaning, he locked himself in the study. Neither of us had a key or the code to the office. Alone in the house, why would he need to lock himself in? And then there's Jasper. If he was the only one there, he'd want Jasper to be able to go in and out of the study."

I took a deep breath. "Was the alarm set? If the alarm was set, then the person had to know that code – probably the same as the one he used for the front door. I don't know how else the person would get into the house unless Ted let them in, in which case he would have locked the study."

"Okay, Mrs. Noth. Thank you for the information."

I stared at the phone. Jillian didn't waste any time. "He thinks you killed Ted? He could have gotten all that information from anyone. He's trying to trip you up, Stacie. You better be careful."

"She's right, Stacie. Stick to the facts as you know them. And don't offer up any information." Wade's advice sounded a lot like Nate's.

The laughter was long forgotten. I made excuses and headed home to Jasper who was probably crossing his legs and starving

CHAPTER 8

Stress permeated the day from the time I woke up, Jasper's sweet kisses the only bright spot. Forcing myself to eat breakfast, I tried a few simple yoga moves before getting dressed. I donned the black sheath once more, pulled my hair up into a bun, and added a touch of blush. Even with the blush, I looked like a ghost.

Jillian arrived and I could tell she had taken care with her appearance knowing the crowd we'd be in. She had on a patterned tunic and long black skirt with heels. At 5'10" she usually avoided the heels, but she stood tall and strong. Her jet black hair was pulled back from her face and she'd even added a touch of makeup.

"You look good, Stacie. Are you ready to deal with this – the funeral, his family, and friends? The whole country club set?"

"I guess. You dress up good. As for Ted, we'd grown apart even before… I felt betrayed. Still I didn't wish him dead."

Jillian patted my arm. "It's okay to mourn for him you know. But be prepared for the onslaught from the society set, not to mention the ogre Hamilton Noth himself."

I refilled Jasper's water dish, indulged in a quick cuddle, and we left for Cunningham's.

Jillian and I had been friends since college, both first generation students a little lost in a college setting. We'd done well academically and muddled through socially. Neither of us was particularly comfortable with the country club set and the superficial niceness. Not to mention the "honey" this and that.

Jillian was taller than me with an athletic build and didn't fit the country version of a southern lady. Certainly, she was not the dainty or submissive type. Ted accepted Jillian as my friend. His father not so much. Mr. Noth was beyond displeased with Jillian as my maid of honor. He wasn't exactly thrilled when I refused to back down either.

Ted never made negative comments about my family or put me down because of my background. Still, dealing with the Noth family was never high on my list of favorite things to do. Mr. Noth made it clear on every occasion that I was not good enough for his son. On more than one occasion, he made snide remarks about my Italian heritage. It was a short ride so I didn't have too much time to dwell on it.

We walked into the funeral hall and I felt my arm yanked from behind. "Stacie, you need to come sit with the family."

I looked at Mr. Noth's grip on my arm, sure I'd have bruises. "Jillian's sitting with me."

He growled and jerked my arm. I wondered if he was going to drag me through the room. Jillian moved a little closer. With her heels, she was his height.

"You don't really want to create a scene, do you?" She whispered but her message was clear.

He glared at her and opened his mouth to say something. He never got to spit it out though.

"Good morning. Is there a problem? Something we didn't take care of?"

"No, Mr. Livingston everything is fine. We were just making our way to our seats."

Mr. Livingston glanced at us and nodded his head. "Good. We'll get started in a few minutes."

Mr. Noth turned back to me. "Let's go." With another glare to Jillian, he added, "You too, Ms. Fleetwood."

Our seats were to the side, the ornate wooden box with Ted's ashes placed in front of our section, but also accessible to others. Mitch was nowhere in sight. Maureen was seated alongside her mother. Both petite and so slim, they looked frail and overcome with grief. The two women held on to each other and sobbed. Mr. Noth sat ramrod straight on his daughter's other side. I recognized Ted's grandparents at the other end of the row. There was no doubt that Mr. Noth took after his father. They stared straight ahead and showed no emotion at all even as people stopped to speak with them.

A presentation of Ted's life played in the front of the hall. A rotating display of images from early childhood into adulthood, in various venues – at school, playing baseball, graduating college, getting his law degree, in his office, on the golf course, at other events. There were pictures of him with his parents, grandparents, and Maureen. Although I had to sit with the family for the sake of appearances, pictures of our wedding hadn't made the cut. In fact, I was not in any of the pictures.

People came up and expressed their condolences to each of us, including Jillian. I stood, needing to expel some nervous energy. Some of the people I knew, some I didn't. No matter. The message was some version of "So sorry. So much of life ahead. Sorry for your loss." Thankfully it was pretty rote or I would have run out of tissues.

"Don't look but the Langfords are here." Jillian whispered in my ear.

Of course I looked. Even dressed in funeral black, eyes red and swollen, Meredith was beautiful. Her long blonde hair glowed and bounced as she walked. She stood proud, her father's arm around her. They moved through the crowd and soon stood in front of me.

I nodded to the Senator and Meredith. He nodded back but kept his arm around his daughter. Distinguished and somber. Meredith pulled me toward her for a hug. She whispered in my ear, "We need to talk. There's something you need to know."

I nodded. Perhaps she didn't think I knew he cheated on her, too. No time to worry about it. People continued to express their condolences until Mr. Livingston announced, "Please be seated as we continue to celebrate Ted's life."

It took a few minutes for everyone to comply and the soft music piped in changed as an additional cue.

Soon Mr. Livingston talked to the crowd and regaled Ted's accomplishments and virtues. I tuned out and scanned the crowd. I spotted O'Hare. Attired in the sports jacket he'd worn the last time I saw him, he was alert to what was happening. He nodded.

Jillian nudged me and directed my attention to Mr. Livingston. "Would anyone else wish to say a few words?"

Mr. Noth took center stage and began with, "The women in Ted's life, his mother, his sister, and his wife, are too overcome with grief. I will speak on their behalf."

He expressed the feelings of loss felt by the family. He then extolled Ted's virtues briefly. He glanced over at our little group as he ended with, "I have faith that the police will quickly bring the murderer to justice." With that, he sat down.

A part of me wanted to stand up and speak for myself, but I realized that would be for me – in defiance of Ted's father – not for Ted. When Mr. Livingston asked if anyone else wished to speak, Mr. Chameux from Ted's law firm said a few words. Not to be outdone, Mr. Jenkins from Noth, Jenkins, and Dantzig spoke of how much Ted had contributed to the community and his work ethic. Then it was over.

The ride to the Noth burial plots at Celestial Gardens was only a few miles. At Mr. Noth's insistence, Jillian pulled in behind the limousine, her silver Accord far from the status of the cars that followed. They ranged from the sporty Continental GT to the more functional Escalade. With the exception of one red Ferrari and Jillian's Accord, all the vehicles were black.

The service at the cemetery was short and somber. The small, ornate wooden box was placed and buried amidst the graves of Noths from prior generations. People milled around, not sure what to do next. Jillian and I escaped.

CHAPTER 9

It was a quiet ride back to town. The burial made it somehow more real – Ted was dead. I replayed the good times in my head, a conscious decision to remember the good rather than the bad. Jillian suggested lunch, but I opted out. I wasn't hungry. I didn't want any company.

She pulled in my driveway. "I can tell you want to be alone. Can I just use the bathroom real quick?"

I gave her shoulder a squeeze. "Of course. And you can say hello to Jasper."

We walked toward the house and Jillian touched my arm. "Stace, we didn't leave your door open."

I started for the door, and she pulled me back. "You can't go in there. What if the burglar is still there?"

I nodded and we got back in the car. Jillian called 9-1-1 and we waited. In only a few minutes, we heard the siren. We walked to the end of the drive when the police car pulled up. I immediately recognized Rick.

As he and another officer approached I heard him say, "You're lead on this one."

The officer nodded and addressed the two of us. "I'm Officer Reardon. You called in a burglary?"

"That was me. We just came home and the door is open. We closed it when we left."

"Okay. Stay here and we'll have a look around."

The two men went into the house. We didn't have to wait long and they came back out. Rick hung back, talking to someone on his phone.

"Ma'am. Officer Murdock said this is your home. Whoever was here is gone now. Before we go in, what time did you leave here this morning?"

"Around 9:30?" I turned to Jillian and she nodded. "Is Jasper alright?"

"Jasper?"

"My dog. You didn't see my dog? I have to find him!" I pushed past him into the house while he tried to talk. There was a mess with books, papers, and dishes scattered, but I didn't care.

"Jasper! Jasper!"

I checked every room including under the beds. Then I ran out to the backyard still calling his name and then back out the front. The two officers were talking to Jillian.

"I have to find Jasper. He doesn't know this neighborhood. He could be hurt, lost."

The officer started to say something and Rick followed me as I ran down the driveway. "You give Reardon the information and I'll search for the dog. What's he look like?"

"He's white, a Maltese. He weighs about 10 lbs."

He took off down to the street, calling for Jasper. I walked back to Reardon and Jillian. "Jasper's lost or kidnapped. I have to find him."

"I called Trina and she and I will both search for him along with the other officer. She took the day off for a doctor appointment. We'll find him, Stacie." She gave me a hug.

Jillian disappeared into the house and came back out with dog treats. A car pulled up and I recognized the car and driver. As usual, she wore a colorful top and skinny jeans. Her reddish brown hair was braided with blue streaks. Even with a day off, she wore makeup and I could smell the patchouli as she gave me a hug.

"Jasper's missing Trina."

"I know, Stacie. Jillie called me. We'll see about Jasper. You deal with the police, okay?"

I nodded. As they walked off, Jillian added, "We'll help you with the mess when we get Jasper home." She and Trina went off in different directions from Rick to cover the neighborhood.

"Mrs. Noth, your friend gave me a run down of your morning. It's possible someone read about the funeral, knew you wouldn't be home, and figured your home would be an easy target. Happens all the time."

I stopped him. "Only there was no notice in the paper and my address wouldn't have been associated anyway. Ted never lived here. I have an unlisted number."

He cocked his head at an angle and opened his mouth just as O'Hare arrived.

"Mrs. Noth. Reardon, everything under control here?"

"Yes, sir. Mrs. Noth hasn't determined if anything is missing as yet."

"I tried to explain to her this happens often with funerals…"

"Given the open investigation into her husband's murder, we have to at least consider this is somehow related."

"Jasper is missing. Rick, Jillian, and Trina are trying to find him. I hope he's alright." My eyes filled up and I swiped my hands across my face.

He scowled. "What's Murdock doing here?"

I followed his line of sight. "Jasper! He found Jasper." I ran toward him and took Jasper into my arms. O'Hare was right behind me.

"Murdock?"

"We got the burglary call. No one else was close by. Reardon is lead."

He nodded. "Mrs. Noth, let's see if you can figure out what they were looking for."

I nodded, and handed Jasper back to Rick. His height and girth compared to Jasper was almost humorous. "I have to call Trina and Jillian to tell them he's found."

An hour and many unanswered questions later, O'Hare and the officers left. Starving, Jillian, Trina, and I sat down at the table to eat sandwiches from Molly's Café, Jasper curled up at my feet. I had no idea why anyone would break in and make a mess of my house. No clue what they thought they'd find at my house.

"Now, Stacie, remind me where you met the tall, dark and handsome man in blue?" Trina asked as she finished her cookie. Single again for a year now, Trina was ready for a new relationship.

"At Creekview Lounge. No big deal. He is good looking though. I know O'Hare had some issue with Rick knowing me. I don't think he was happy to see Rick here. Of course, O'Hare's handsome too." I shrugged.

Trina nodded and whistled. "You can say that again. Do they all hang out at Creekview?"

"Enough, we have work to do," Jillian reminded us.

Then we cleaned up the mess. We filled my trash can and then some. We continued the discussion as we worked. Jasper lay in the new dog bed and watched us.

"You need better locks on your doors, Stacie. A deadbolt at least."

"You're probably right, Jillian. But whoever did this won't be back – they know I don't have whatever they wanted, right?"

Jillian shook her head. "I wouldn't be too sure of that. They only know they didn't find it – or they did and you don't realize it's missing. Whatever it is, they believed you hid it. Was Ted ever here? Maybe he hid something while you got a drink or used the bathroom or something."

"He was never here. His father was never here."

"Did either of them have the address?"

"Yes. Ted had the address to forward mail. When I moved out I tacked it on the bulletin board in the kitchen. And it was on the divorce papers – that's how the police knew where I lived."

"Stacie, maybe that's how the person who did this knew where you lived, too."

I nodded to Jillian. That would make sense.

"Are you okay staying here by yourself? You want to stay with me and Wade?"

"I'm fine. O'Hare said he'd request additional surveillance in the neighborhood for a few days. And besides, I have Jasper."

We all laughed at that and Jasper, now asleep on my lap, didn't so much as budge.

"Thanks for all your help cleaning up and lunch and everything."

Finally done, I walked my friends out with hugs and more thanks. Taking out the last of the trash, the neighbor across the street shook his head at me. Obviously all the police activity would lower the property value. Back inside, I took stock of what needed to be replaced. After locking up and checking the doors a second time, Jasper and I took a nap. I'd see about getting better locks another time.

CHAPTER 10

My phone rang as I got back from an early morning yoga class. Yet another unknown number.

"Stacie? This is Veronica at CO&N."

I was a little surprised to hear from anyone from Ted's office and especially his administrative assistant. I remembered her as an attractive red head with a great figure. Even in our early days of wedded bliss, I wondered about their relationship and his choice of someone young with no paralegal experience.

"Hi, Veronica."

"First, let me express my condolences. I saw you at the funeral, but didn't want to intrude."

"Thank you, Veronica. And thank you for calling." I didn't remember seeing her, but then I probably didn't notice a lot of people.

"Well, the reason I'm calling... I need to give you the box of Ted's things from his office. There are pictures and such you might want. Otherwise, the whole box will go to recycling."

"Of course. When could I come by and get the box?"

"I... I don't think that's a good idea. Can you meet me at Starbucks? The one on Hyde Street around 12:30?"

Not having anything scheduled, I agreed. Even though I couldn't imagine that I would want anything in the box, a part of me was feeling nostalgic. Certainly, anything proprietary they would have kept. I did mundane tasks before I left to meet her, including a grocery list. That would be my first stop after Starbucks.

Not surprising, Starbucks at lunchtime was packed. I waited in line, glancing around for Veronica or for a table to open up. My Skinny Mocha in hand, I found a table and sat down.

The first thing I noticed about Veronica when she walked in was the baby bump. I obviously wasn't up on Ted's office gossip. She was still attractive and she glowed. Somehow she also looked tired at the same time.

"Hi. Thanks for meeting me." She lowered herself into the chair slowly with a groan.

"When are you due?"

"Three weeks and that's not soon enough." She chuckled. "As much as I like the apple berry here, I can't wait to have a good strong cup of coffee. And to be able to see my feet."

"I could have come to the office for the box, you know."

"Yes and no. I wanted to talk to you and that wouldn't work in the office. I know things were on the outs – between you and Ted, I mean. As his admin, I knew every time he talked to someone and usually what it was about. Mr. Armstead's calls usually had him riled up."

I didn't know what to say. Nate always dealt with Mr. Armstead, Ted's attorney, not me. "What about you? Did they find a place for you – assuming you want to work, that is?"

It was like a cloud passed over her face, her mouth set. She sat up and with a deep breath she explained.

"Spencer Krumm moved into Ted's office this morning and the assumption was that I went with the office. I managed to get the office cleaned out of Ted's personal effects before he arrived. Hence the box of stuff that doesn't belong to CO&N I have for you."

The human resource counselor in me picked up the tension. "What are your plans for the job, Veronica?"

"My original plan was to take my leave time and return to the office. I'd already set up the temp to keep things organized for Ted. Honestly, with our bills, not working isn't an option and CO&N pays me well." Her gaze shifted downward.

"But?"

"I'll be seeking another position. Ted could flirt with the best of them – sorry – but he kept his hands to himself. His comments were light. What kind of idiot makes a pass at …" She glanced away before she continued, "an obviously very pregnant and married woman?" She took a deep breath and looked down at the table.

"Did he touch you inappropriately? Did you report his behavior? That's harassment, you know."

"Yes, I know. No, I didn't report it. The last woman who worked for him did and she was told she 'must have misinterpreted' his actions. He's pretty powerful and very aggressive in getting what he wants. Including Ted's office."

"Wait. Wasn't Ted up for partner? Or would he change offices with that?"

"It was between Ted and Krumm from everything I heard. Ted had the smooth and the social skills; Krumm had the aggression and drive. Lots of meetings behind closed doors. Some of the paralegals joked that it had to be Ted so it would be 'COR&N' – a little 'corny' you know."

"But now it will be 'COK&N" or "CON&K?"

"Jury's out. They announced that Spencer would move into Ted's office, however they are postponing any decisions on partner until all the pending cases have been resolved. That in itself is weird. Krumm wasn't too happy about that. In the meantime he's bent on showing them he should get the position."

Giving herself a shake, she continued, "Anyway I packed up Ted's stuff and wanted to give it to you."

"Okay. You said you wanted to talk to me, too?"

"Yes. I don't know if it means anything. Ted was on edge the last few weeks. Yeah, the pressure of the possible partnership and your divorce, but I think something else was going on. I just don't know what."

"Have the police talked to you? Asked you any questions?"

"Not me. And not at the office that I know of."

"That seems odd to me. I guess they have their reasons." I shrugged but I was definitely going to talk to a certain detective.

"Were any of his clients angry with him or upset with his representation? I mean I know you couldn't tell me who or what it was about, but if that's a possibility, that a client had a motive, the police should know."

"Nothing out of the ordinary. As far as I know, his clients were all pleased. He schmoozed them all. Chameux got on his case sometimes about how long it took him to close the deal or get the client's desired effect, but the results were always good."

I nodded. That was the Ted I remembered. He'd chisel away at the resistance to get the prize, always with a smile. Even convince someone that his solution was the one they wanted all along. I finished my coffee.

"Shall we? I'll walk with you to where ever you parked to get the box so you don't have to carry it."

We got up and headed out the door. As we walked down the street, she talked about the baby and the preparations. At the walk light, we moved to cross the street and she doubled over. I pulled her back toward the sidewalk as someone yelled "Watch out!" and two strong arms grabbed both of us. We were pulled back onto the sidewalk. A black Cadillac Escalade screamed by. Veronica started to straighten up.

The man who'd helped us get out of the way let go and turned toward us. "Are you okay? That jerk almost hit you." He appeared to be a construction worker from his t-shirt, jeans, and tool belt.

"Yes, I think we're okay. Veronica?"

"I... I think..." and she doubled over again. I held on to her, glad she was shorter than me.

"Call 9-1-1. I think she may be in labor."

The man paled, pulled out his phone and made the call, at the same time moving us both further from the street. He stayed with us until the police and paramedics arrived. He talked with the police while the paramedics took care of Veronica. She was able to get in the ambulance with their help and they assured me they'd notify her husband.

"The box?"

"It'll wait. Take care of yourself and baby Elle."

The police officers and the man surrounded me as the ambulance sped away.

"Ma'am, can you tell us what happened?"

"Huh? She went into labor I guess. She said she was due in three weeks."

One officer looked at the man and his eyebrows arched. The man turned to me. "Tell him about the car that ran the light."

"Oh, okay. We were about to cross the street. The signal said we could go and we'd taken a few steps into the street. That's when Veronica gasped, grabbed her belly, and doubled over. I pulled her back to the sidewalk with this man's help as a black Escalade sped by us. At least I think it was an Escalade."

The officer and the man exchanged glances. "Did you notice anything else about the car?"

"Heck no, I was too busy trying to keep the two of us upright."

"Can I get your name and address in case we have any other questions?"

I complied and thanked the man. The man shook his head and walked away.

As I finished my errands and drove home, it occurred to me that I'd had more interaction with Beckman Springs police in the past week than in my entire life. At home, I fed Jasper and called the hospital. Veronica had been admitted and that was all they could tell me. It dawned on me that we probably had a lot in common. Maybe there was an opening at Foster's Insurance Group she'd be interested in.

CHAPTER 11

The phone rang as the timer went off for the lasagna. Another unknown number, something all too frequent the past few days. At least nobody was trying to sell me something or get me to vote for someone.

"Hello."

"Mrs. Noth. Detective O'Hare here. I have a few questions and I was wondering if I could stop by and get these cleared up."

"Sure. When did you want to come by?"

"I'm in the neighborhood, so about five minutes?"

"Fine. See you then."

I turned the oven off and pulled the lasagna out. It needed to cool anyway. There wasn't much in my neighborhood, so I didn't think it was happenstance for O'Hare to be in the neighborhood. I met the detective and Officer Flatt at the door.

"Come on in."

I sat down on the sofa. I motioned to the two chairs and they sat. Flatt opened a bottle of water he'd brought in. O'Hare leaned forward. He looked haggard and his hair fell onto his face, traces of gray showing.

"Thank you for agreeing to talk with us. We are trying to tie up some loose ends and I have some questions for you."

"No recorder this time?"

"Not this time." He pulled out his notebook. "What can you tell me about the firm Ted worked for? Who he got along with, who he didn't."

I wondered why he kept asking me these questions, but decided to play along. Anything if it helped solve Ted's murder so I could move on with my life.

"CO&N specializes in business law. Ted got his degree from Brown in business law, but he worked with cybersecurity, intellectual property, and technology law more than others in the firm. Chameux encouraged these activities given the increasing emphasis on technology and cybersecurity in major businesses. With his own interests in technology and games, Ted was a natural."

"That's right. He had all that technology at the house. Did he work for a lot of corporations or only one?"

"As far as I know – I've been out of the loop for six months – he worked for different corporations depending on the situation to be addressed."

"Do you know any of the corporations?"

"Detective, we never socialized with the people he represented, at least not on an individual basis. We occasionally socialized with other junior partners or at a firm function to honor someone, or the holidays, you know. I mean Ted may have had dinners or lunches with a CEO or other representative to discuss problems, but I wouldn't have been involved. He didn't talk about his clients by name – ever. That doesn't mean he didn't get frustrated and cuss them occasionally."

"I see. What about the people at CO&N? I have a note here he was up for partner?"

"That's what I understood. Now I don't know. Veronica said it wasn't certain."

"I'm sorry. Who is Veronica and why wasn't it certain?"

"Veronica was Ted's admin assistant. I had coffee with her today and she said it hadn't been decided. It was between him and Spencer Krumm."

"So you and Veronica are friends, and you're only learning this now?"

"No. Veronica and I aren't friends. She called and asked me to meet her so she could give me a box with Ted's personal effects from the office. That's when she told me about Krumm and how he'd moved into Ted's office, taken over his cases, and such. Ted never mentioned him and I've never met him."

"And what was in the box?"

"I don't know. She said pictures and stuff. She's pregnant and went into labor before I could get the box from her."

His mouth dropped. I could see he thought I was making the whole thing up. Maybe I was still a suspect after all.

"If you don't believe me, you can check it out. We had to call 9-1-1. The paramedics came and an officer took my statement about a car that ran a red light."

O'Hare nodded to Flatt, who immediately stepped over to the door, mumbling.

"Anyone other than this Krumm person who might not have liked your husband?"

"Not that I know of. He worked with paralegals mostly and he could be critical. But he was adept at making people feel good when he wanted something. Veronica would know better than me if anyone had an issue with him." I glared at him and added, "She said no one has been to talk to them or ask them anything."

"In due time."

Flatt re-joined us and cleared his throat.

"What did you find out?"

"She's telling the truth about the lady going into labor. And the car going through the red light. She left out the part about a Mr. Allegro. He was sure the car was heading for the two women – not only going very fast, through a red light, but a little too close to the curb."

"What?"

"You didn't notice anything like that Mrs. Noth?"

"All I noticed was Veronica's gasp and her doubling over. I didn't even see the car until we were back on the sidewalk."

"Okay. Mr. Allegro may have an overactive imagination. Can you think of anyone else your husband didn't get along with or who might have something to gain from his death?"

I chuckled. "Mitch for sure. If Ted could have filed charges against him, he would have. He even contacted the police and a lawyer. They all said the same thing – Maureen had to press charges, not him. Obviously, the secret is out now."

O'Hare scowled and then nodded for me to go on.

"Meredith or her father, or the boyfriend or husband of the new cleaning lady? I don't know." I shrugged. "I have no idea who Ted may have angered in the past six months. In all honesty, we didn't spend a lot of time together for the six months before that. Veronica could give you any dirt from the office."

I paused to think. "Neighbors? I bet Jerilyn Walters, the neighbor who called about Ted, could tell you about comings and goings from the house. She was the neighborhood busy body. Not to mention whatever information is in the logs from the gatehouse or the surveillance footage."

O'Hare shook his head and grimaced. "Apparently, the management decided it was so well known there was surveillance, they didn't need to keep the tapes, and sometimes the guard forgot to turn on the recording system."

My mouth dropped. So much for feeling secure in a gated community with the best of technology.

"We still haven't located the backup drive you mentioned. Any idea where he might have put it?"

I shook my head. "The safe?"

O'Hare shrugged and stood. Flatt moved toward the door. "Okay. I only have one other question. Any chance someone from your family…?"

I laughed at him. "Mr. Noth suggested it right? He tried to convince Ted that marrying me was marrying into the mafia because of the Italian background. To the best of my knowledge there is no mafia connection. My father was overjoyed when I told him I'd left Ted, but he wouldn't have killed him."

"Is your father local?"

"No, he's not. He lives in New Jersey. I'm sure you can check on his whereabouts. He manages a construction company in conjunction with one of the builders in New Jersey and New York. Lately he spends most of his time in upstate New York. Pretty handy around the house, but not a murderer." I didn't mention the lady friend that was part of the reason for his upstate destination these days.

"I had to ask. Good night, Mrs. Noth. Be safe."

CHAPTER 12

The calls from O'Hare were becoming so commonplace I wasn't surprised to hear from him again, even on a Saturday. Someone was delivering the box from Ted's office. I guessed it was like a bandaid, better to get it over with.

The doorbell rang and I opened the door assuming it would be the detective. Instead, a large man, with red stringy hair in a comb over and a ruddy complexion stood on my doorstep. He reeked of alcohol and I took a step back instinctively.

"What? Who are you?"

"Spencer Krumm. From Ted's office. You're looking good." He checked me out in an obvious and exaggerated fashion, wiggling his eyebrows. Ewww.

"Excuse me, but why are you here?"

"Now Stacie, you're not being very friendly. Don't you think you should invite me in?" He didn't wait for an answer and moved forward into my comfort zone. I moved back in reaction and he slammed the door.

"I'll ask you again. Why are you here?" I raised my voice. He was twice my size but I didn't care. Jasper growled and I picked him up.

"Stacie, I wanted to express my condolences. Isn't that what friends do?"

"Fine. Thank you. But we're not friends. I've never met you. And you can leave now."

"Not so quick. Ted and I were working together on some cases and some of the notes seem to be missing. Do you have those notes?"

"Huh? Why would I have Ted's notes? We've been separated for six months."

"Someone cleaned out his office. Are you telling me it wasn't you?"

"I haven't been to his office in at least a year. Probably Opinsky has his notes, or Chameux. They wouldn't even be meaningful to me." I didn't mention Veronica. It would make sense that Veronica would give all the proprietary stuff, including notes, to the senior partner in charge.

The doorbell sounded and I took advantage of Krumm's hesitation to yell, "Coming, be right there," as I bolted past him for the door. Rick stood there with the box. Squelching my surprise, I adlibbed.

"Officer Murdock, how nice of you to come by. Thank you so much for boxing up all of Jasper's toys and food. Come on in. You can put the box in the kitchen."

Rick glanced from me to Krumm and walked in.

"Kitchen is that way. I do appreciate all you've done and how frequently you stop by."

Rick hesitated, then walked past me to the kitchen.

He was barely out of sight and Krumm quipped, "If he's coming by, he has ulterior motives. You're one hot woman."

He started to move in my direction and I backed up. Jasper growled and bared his teeth. I'd never seen him behave like that before. Jasper had good instincts though.

"Like I said Mr. Krumm, I don't have anything from Ted's office, no notes on cases, nothing. So you can just leave."

Rick joined us and stood beside me.

"Officer Murdock. And you are?"

"Spencer Krumm, Esquire. A colleague of Ted's. Just stopped by to express my condolences to the widow, Officer." His voice sneered at the end, his disdain apparent.

"Didn't I hear her suggest you leave? Did I hear wrong?" He glanced at me but fixed his glare on Krumm.

"I guess in her grief, she isn't up for much company. Maybe I'll catch you another time, Stacie." He leered at me again, but thankfully he left.

I stumbled as the door closed and Rick guided me to the sofa. "Take a minute, while I call O'Hare."

He stepped outside. By the time he returned, I had calmed down. Nestled in my lap, Jasper's mere presence had a soothing effect. His tail beat me as he wagged it in response to Rick.

"O'Hare should be here in a few minutes, Mrs. Noth."

"Please, call me Stacie. You have no idea how glad I am you showed up when you did. He scared me."

"I could see that – he's definitely not subtle. Can I get you something? How's Jasper doing?"

"No, thank you. Jasper's good and great therapy. I'm forgetting my manners. Please sit down. Can I get you anything?"

He shook his head as he sat. We talked about the weather and my job in HR until the detective arrived. Rick answered the door and both joined me in the living room.

"Mrs. Noth. Are you okay?"

"Please, call me Stacie, Detective. I'm fine now. Why don't you both sit down?"

They complied and O'Hare started the conversation. "Murdock here said he arrived with the box from Ted's office and someone else was here. Who was he and what did he want?"

"I answered the door thinking it was you. Only he was there and obnoxious. It was Spencer Krumm, the attorney in competition with Ted for partnership. He pushed his way in and accused me of cleaning out Ted's office. From the smell, he'd been drinking. He asked about notes that he says are missing."

O'Hare glanced over at Rick and then back to me. "What did you tell him?"

"I told him I didn't have anything from Ted's office and didn't know anything about cases they were working on together. I suggested he check with the senior partners. For the record, Ted never worked on a project with other partners – he had his paralegal team. Krumm should have had his own team if he's up for partner."

"Anything else?"

"Veronica was right. That man is slime and sexist and … I need a shower just from his innuendos." I shuddered and Jasper jumped off my lap.

"Murdock, what happened when you arrived?"

"Mrs. Noth launched into this whole thing about Jasper's toys and food and directed me to the kitchen. She was practically jumping out of her skin. She asked him to leave. He wasn't taking the not so subtle hint. I restated her request – after introducing myself – and he complied."

"I'm afraid he'll be back." I shuddered again.

O'Hare turned to Rick and I caught the slight nod. Rick thought he'd be back too.

"So someone trashes Ted's house, presumably trying to find something or just angry. They didn't steal anything. Then someone does the same here. You're with Ted's Assistant to get a box of stuff from his office and you almost get run down. Now Krumm is nosing around asking about notes Ted might have had. I think we need to see what's in that box you just brought in, Murdock, and then the one Veronica has."

"You mean, that's not the one from Veronica?"

"No ma'am. We boxed up the papers in his home office and safe. I'm hoping you can make some sense of it. Identify what might or might not be important."

"Oh, so you got the safe open. Did you find the external hard drive?"

"Afraid not. And if I were a betting man, I'd bet that's where whatever Krumm wants will be found."

Rick brought the box into the living area and placed it on the coffee table. I opened it slowly, half expecting something to jump out. On top was our wedding picture. My eyes teared up and I put it off to the side. There were a lot of papers I could identify. The pet policy on Jasper and his rabies certificate I put with the picture. Ted's life insurance policy went in a different pile. There was one for me too. Same pile. Then pages and pages of handwritten statements with lines and letters that seemed unconnected. I stared at them until O'Hare cleared his throat.

"Any idea what those mean?"

"I'm not sure. Almost look like the logic puzzles we used to do – like he was trying to connect events and people and things, but not able to make all the connections fit. He tried multiple sequences and combinations. This one's circled and this one has a question mark. The rest are crossed out, so he must have gotten the solution down to these two and decided on this one. I have no idea what the letters stand for so it's hard to make sense of it." I handed the stack to O'Hare.

"Could it be one of the games he played?" he asked.

"I guess it's possible, but for most online and video games there's a blog or website or online group that can help beat a level. I can't see him trying some 20 different solutions. He could just go online and find the way around the game. Ted was techie with a capital 'T.' If there was a way to do this through technology, he wouldn't have been doing it by hand."

"Maybe that's what Krumm wanted, not realizing it doesn't make sense to anyone else?" Rick's suggested.

"Maybe those are related to a case Krumm ended up with and he can't make sense of them either. Unfortunately, the only time Ted ever talked to me about a case was if it was a game and the issue was copyright infringement. He'd have me play a game and write down all the levels and what was required to see if it matched his analysis."

"Or it would make sense to him, but not us. I think we need to get the other box and talk to Veronica." O'Hare's shoulders slumped.

"I checked on Veronica yesterday and she'd been admitted. I was going to check and maybe go visit today after stopping at Cornerstone."

O'Hare nodded and then stood. "Okay if I take these?"

"Sure. Who do I give Ted's insurance policy to? Mr. Trichter?"

Both men stared at me and Rick shook his head.

"Who's the beneficiary?" O'Hare asked.

"I don't know. I assume these are through CO&N and mine was probably cancelled already. Veronica may know about them. I'll ask her."

They both nodded and I walked them to the door. O'Hare hung back as Rick walked to his car.

"How did Krumm know where you live?"

"No idea. Unless he saw it at Ted's house."

O'Hare nodded. That could put him at the house the night he was killed or any time in the past six months.

"We'll continue surveillance and be more obvious about it. If you see or hear anything out of the ordinary, call 9-1-1. Keep your doors locked and don't open the door without checking to see who it is. Let me know if you find out anything from Veronica."

I agreed and quickly locked the door. I fed Jasper, put the papers and wedding picture in the guest room, and called the hospital. Veronica was still there. I could stop in at Cornerstone and still make it before visiting hours ended.

CHAPTER 13

Cornerstone Community Women's Shelter was on the border of Beckman Springs and Reston for now. No address was printed anywhere. There was no sign on the main road. You had to know to turn down Liberation Lane. There was no street sign, only the dirt road named by the shelter staff.

It was a good two miles before the large house loomed off to the side. Unassuming, with a front porch, a swing and slide, and two cars. To those who didn't know better, it was a family's country home instead of a shelter for battered women and their children.

I beeped my horn and then approached the front door. Shawna opened the door and pulled me into a hug. She was the resident manager and a survivor. She kept track of what was going on and who came and went. She'd been with Cornerstone for at least seven years and this was her second location. It was my second as well.

"I've been thinking about you since I saw the news about Ted's murder. How are you, Stacie?"

"Good. How's everybody here? Full house?" We moved into the house and the office. It smelled of cinnamon and I spotted the Scentsy plug in. Last week it had been vanilla.

"Come in and have a seat. We have two new guests. Dr. Hanreddy's been by for one of them. She's in bad shape. Her sister called someone who called someone, and Lyla went and picked her up. She'll need some support, but not yet."

"Police called?"

"Not yet. She's saying no. And not likely to happen. She won't even tell us her name. From her clothes and manners, she's the wife of someone important. Money can't buy everything, but manages to buy silence. For now, she's safe and that's what's most important. The longer she stays, the harder it will be for her to go back."

"And the other one?"

"Trish isn't talking much. Police picked her up but she wouldn't say what happened. The victim services worker called the hotline and Lyla picked her up. She's still not talking much. She has some old injuries and Dr. Hanreddy thinks she has a concussion. She seems young and old at the same time. More street wise and rough though."

"Okay. Well, bring me around so I can touch base with the women from last week and at least be a friendly face to these two. I didn't want to cancel my visit, but I'm not really up to much."

Shawna nodded and we walked through the house. Lyla came over and gave me a hug. She was one of the people who brought women to Cornerstone when they couldn't go home or decided they'd had enough. She was a big woman and I'd heard stories of her knocking out a man when he tried to stop her a time or two.

After an hour of being upbeat and supportive, providing positive comments and encouragement, I was on my way. It still surprised me that battering didn't know any social barriers.

I headed back to town and managed to get to the hospital in time to see Veronica. The nurses directed me to her room. I walked in to find a man holding her hand and O'Hare.

"Hi. Should I come back? I don't want to interrupt." I started to back up.

"No, no, Stacie, please stay. This is my husband, Andy Gomez." She turned to him and added, "Stacie is who took care of me yesterday."

Andy held Veronica's hand and the picture was Hallmark quality for the loving husband. He was an attractive man and the two seemed to go together. No doubt baby Elle would be a red head. Instead of Veronica's blue eyes, Andy had brown eyes. Time would tell on Elle's eyes.

"Glad I could help. How are you and baby Elle?"

"Good. Good. It wasn't labor after all. I've been binging on all kinds of fruit, and well, I paid the price. Won't do that again for sure."

Embarrassed, she added, "I think you know the detective…" Her gaze shifted to him.

I nodded.

"Mrs. Noth – Stacie. Mrs. Gomez noticed the black car, too."

"Good thing you and that man got us back off the road. That car was driving awful close to the curb." Her husband nodded his thanks and squeezed her hand.

Her comment made me wonder if maybe Mr. Allegro was right after all. So was the driver after her or me? O'Hare peered at me but didn't say anything. No one did. I finally broke the awkward silence.

"I'm going to see if I can find a coffee machine. Can I get anyone anything?"

Nobody answered and I hesitated. O'Hare cleared his throat. "Mr. Gomez, would you mind if I spoke to your wife for a few minutes? Perhaps you could help Stacie find the coffee?"

Veronica nodded and we both went in search of caffeine. We made small talk and took our time getting back. Andy talked a lot about baby Elle and how excited and scared he was that it was almost time. By the time we returned to Veronica's room, O'Hare was gone.

"Everything alright, Ronni?" Andy asked as he took his place by her side.

She nodded to him and then turned to me. "He had a lot of questions about Ted and Spencer Krumm." She looked back to Andy, "Can you arrange to get that box out of my trunk and to Stacie tonight or tomorrow? He thinks maybe there's something in there that might help the investigation."

"I can drop it off at your house when I leave here tonight. I just need your address."

"That would be fine." I pulled out a piece of paper and jotted down my address.

"When do you get out of here? Will you be going back to work?"

"I think… I'm hoping my doctor will suggest I stay home and not go back. That was the detective's idea. He seemed to think it would be best – safer."

I did a double take and it occurred to me that O'Hare was taking Mr. Allegro's notion that someone was trying to hit us seriously. "That is probably for the best, and I'm sure you have a lot to do before baby Elle arrives."

Andy squeezed her shoulder and smiled down at her. She smiled back.

"Well, I think I better be going. Please keep me posted and, Andy, I'll see you later."

CHAPTER 14

Whoever said you shouldn't shop when hungry was right. In a quick stop at the grocery store, I not only picked up healthy foods, I filled the buggy with a couple packages of cookies, chips, and a half-gallon of Rocky Road. Depending on what was in the box, comfort food might be needed. Take-out from Luigi's and I was homeward bound. At one point, I spotted a black Escalade behind me. It turned off and I chided myself that I was getting paranoid. There were a lot of black Escalades around Beckman Springs.

Jasper was excited to see me and I got him outside and fed. Everything put away, my dinner of chicken fettuccini hit the spot. I'd just cleaned up the dishes and put the leftovers in the fridge, when Jasper growled and I heard someone or something outside the back door. It sounded like wood breaking. Jasper barked and growled some more. It reminded me of his reaction to Krumm.

I dropped to the floor so I couldn't be seen from the kitchen window. A quick glance at the back door confirmed that it was locked. My purse was close enough for me to grab my phone. Jasper running and barking made it hard for me to hear if anyone was out there, but this wasn't his typical behavior. I dialed 9-1-1 and the dispatcher took my information.

The dispatcher kept me on the line. I heard a man yell something but I couldn't understand what he said, only that it seemed to come from the front of the house, not the back. Then the sirens, increasing in volume as they drew near.

"Mrs. Noth, the officers have arrived at your home. Please wait until they have secured the area."

I thanked her and waited. It was quiet but I could see the glow from the flashing lights through the kitchen windows. Dead bolts were definitely on the to-do list now. Maybe an alarm system and motion detectors. I'd ask Wade to install them. My phone rang.

"Mrs. Noth. Detective O'Hare here. Murdock should be knocking on your door any minute. Area is cleared and I'm on my way."

I mumbled "Okay" and he disconnected. Almost on cue, someone knocked on the front door. I peered through the hole and recognized Rick. I opened the door, but he didn't move forward. He stepped back.

"Mrs. Noth – Stacie. Can you tell us what happened and who this man is?"

I followed Rick's gaze and saw a man down on the ground. As I moved closer, I looked from him to Rick. "That's Andy Gomez – Veronica's husband. He was coming over to drop off the box tonight. Is he alright?"

Two paramedics were by his side and talking, but so softly I couldn't hear at first.

"You're okay. You're okay. Relax. We're here to help you. Can you tell us what happened?"

"I pulled into the driveway and saw a shadow around the corner of the house. I got out of the car and yelled at the person. Next thing I know, it was like when I played football and got sacked. Down I went."

Andy tried to sit up and the paramedic stopped him. "Let's do this slowly." The two of them helped him sit up, then waited a few minutes. Then he was standing.

"I'm Officer Murdock. Can you tell me anything about the person who knocked you down?"

"Officer, as you can see I'm no lightweight – normally I run around 190. Somehow I've topped the 200 mark with my wife's pregnancy. Sympathy cravings." He chuckled before he continued. "This guy was over 6 foot and outweighed me by about 50. Smelled of something I can't quite place."

"You mean like aftershave?"

"No or at least not one I recognized. More medicinal?"

One of the paramedics cleared his throat. "Mr. Gomez are you all set or do you need a ride to the hospital?"

"I'm fine. Thanks."

They turned to Rick and he nodded. "You're all set."

As they departed, O'Hare joined all of us. Rick filled him in on what had happened. Rick, the officer riding with him, and O'Hare all grabbed flashlights.

"Mr. Gomez, you sure you're alright?" At his nod, O'Hare continued. "Can you show us where you first saw the man who decked you?"

"Of course." He walked with the three officers to the side of the house. They all disappeared around the corner and Andy came back.

"Let me get that box for you." He went to his car and returned with the box.

I opened the door, snatching Jasper as he tried to dart out. "Come on in. You can put it on the table and have a seat. Are you sure you're all right? Let me get you a water."

Andy sat down and immediately Jasper was in his lap. Grabbing four bottles of water, I returned to the main living area as a single knock came to the door. I immediately opened the door. O'Hare and Rick rolled their eyes. The other officer didn't react.

"Do not open the door without verifying who is there." O'Hare barked.

I nodded, handed them waters, and waved the three of them in. "What did you find? Anything?"

"It's pretty dark out there but nothing looked or smelled out of the ordinary. I'll have someone come back and check again in the morning. Mr. Gomez, could what you smelled have been alcohol?"

"Hmm... Possibly. I'm not a big drinker. It wasn't anything obvious like kerosene or gasoline. It was strong enough though I smelled it just before he tackled me."

"Did you notice any cars on the street near here?"

Andy shrugged. "Yeah, there were a few cars here and there, but nothing stood out. Sorry. Anything else?" He stood up.

"I'll be in touch if we need anything else."

"Thanks for bringing the box over. I'll give Veronica a call next week to see how she's doing."

I walked him to the door. "You take care, Stacie." He shook his head and left.

The three men were still there along with the box. I chuckled at the sight of Jasper, now curled up in Rick's lap, a little envious of the little dog.

O'Hare cleared his throat. "Feeling a bit like Pandora?"

I nodded and opened the box. As with the one from his home office, the first things were photographs. Of the two of us, of me, of Jasper, and of his parents. Unframed were some more photographs. All of Maureen. I handed them to O'Hare.

"These are probably the same ones that were in the envelope, but if anybody's keeping the evidence in case she ever presses charges…"

He took the photos and scowled. As he passed them to the other two, I listened to a chorus of growls and groans, scowling faces all around.

I offered, "You know, Mitch Dantzig fits the description. He's easily 250 and over 6 foot. He played football too. And he drinks."

"But what would he be looking for? Why would he be outside your house? As far as he knows, we have all the pictures we'd need." He handed the photos back to me.

I shrugged and continued to go through the box. There were some file folders from our vacations – Barcelona, Calgary, London. A file for insurance. I handed them to O'Hare.

"Not sure how any of these relate. The insurance one is more information on the policies and renewals. According to this, I'm the beneficiary on Ted's policy and he's the beneficiary on mine. I guess that gives me motive but I didn't even know these existed, and he may have changed the beneficiary in the past six months."

O'Hare didn't say a word and Rick stared at the ceiling. The other officer became more alert, eyes wide when he saw the value of Ted's policy. Half a million is a pretty good motive for murder.

"Nothing else in there related to the handwritten stuff we found in his study? Or connected to any of his projects or Krumm?"

I continued through the file folders of our vacations, flashing back to better times. One file wasn't labeled. Inside were pages of transactions. I handed them to O'Hare.

"Here. This one is a listing of cases or dates and coded information. Ted's written Krumm's name on it. Come to think of it, I'm surprised you didn't see similar reports for Ted in his home office. No idea why he'd have Krumm's though."

O'Hare nodded. "We can ask them to provide whatever records they have. These accounts are all by number so privilege shouldn't apply. Maybe Ted was worried Krumm was working some of his accounts?"

"Sorry, no clue. Wait. Let me see that again. If these were cases, I'd expect to see a column with the hours by month."

O'Hare scrunched his eyebrow and Rick's left eyebrow went up. Then he studied the ceiling some more.

"Part of my job in HR is to work with the Employee Assistance Program. I log cases something like this – all in code to protect the employee. My role is more crisis intervention and referral. That's all I can do with my Bachelor's in Social Work. For each incident, I have to track the amount of time I spend working with the employee. So usually that's the initial meeting and referral for services as needed, followed by at least one follow-up visit to see how the person is doing. My log would look like this but would have a column that effectively tracked billable hours. Now, my time isn't actually billed, but Ted's and Krumm's certainly would be."

"That makes sense. What else could this be then?"

I shook my head, but I had an idea. It was time to check in with Veronica about the woman she said complained about Krumm. Not sure if it made sense, I opted not to share it with O'Hare yet.

"Krumm fits the description Gomez provided. He's about my height but eats much better. Definitely over the 250 mark," Rick pointed out.

"And he reeked of alcohol when he was here. Probably hadn't changed from the night before." I shivered as I remembered our meeting.

I set aside the box. Later, I'd move it to my home office – otherwise called the second bedroom and shred whatever wasn't needed.

"Any chance I could make a copy of that log? Maybe something will come to me."

O'Hare shrugged. I took the page and used my printer to make a copy. O'Hare, Rick, and the other officer were standing when I returned to the living room. They tried to convince me to stay somewhere else for the night. I refused. I didn't want to put anyone out or put them in danger. Besides I was sure the turf war between Jillian's cat, Meow, and Jasper would not be pretty.

CHAPTER 15

I opened the door cautiously to get the morning paper and scanned the street and front yard. I spotted an older Mustang across the street I didn't recognize. Closing the door and locking it, calling the police department to check on the car was an option.

It occurred to me to just walk out there and see if anyone was in the car. Then I remembered Andy knocked out on the driveway. I paced back and forth while I drank my coffee, sneaking a peek out the window each time I crossed it. Call or don't call.

Jasper barked and that decided it. I called and reported a strange car on the street and asked if someone could check it out. A few minutes later, my doorbell rang and Jasper barked some more. I peeked out and it was Rick with Flatt.

"Good morning?" Flatt smirked and Rick looked a mess in jeans and a t-shirt. He immediately picked up Jasper, which at least shut him up.

"Mrs. Noth, I responded to your request to check on the car out there…" Flatt pointed out to the street and snorted. "It's Officer Murdock's car, ma'am."

Rick rubbed his eyes. At least that explained why he wasn't exactly on top of things this morning.

"Uh. Thank you Officer Flatt. I guess there's no problem after all. Can I get either of you a cup of coffee?"

"Not me, ma'am. I'll just go deal with real criminals." Flatt shook his head and let himself out.

"Coffee?"

Rick smiled. He followed me into the kitchen.

"Sorry if I scared you. After last night, I was concerned with your safety. I probably should have told you I'd be out there."

"I don't know what to say. Any other time, I probably wouldn't have paid attention to a car out there. But you must not have gotten any sleep."

He nodded and took the coffee. We chatted for a few minutes and despite the caffeine, his head drooped.

"I think I better go. Sleep sounds real good. Thanks for the coffee."

"Thank you."

As I opened the door to let him out, my father stepped forward.

"Stacie."

"Hi, Dad. This is Rick Murdock. He's one of the police officers working on Ted's murder." As if that would explain Rick's appearance or why he was leaving my house first thing in the morning.

"Mr. Maroni. It's nice to meet you. After the incident last night, I watched the house overnight to be sure Stacie was safe." He pointed to his car on the street. "I need to get some sleep, so I'll be going."

Smart man. He didn't waste any time walking past my father. That left me to deal with the questions.

"What incident, Stacie? I came down because I was worried about you."

"Come on in and have some coffee. I'll tell you all about it."

I gave him a hug and he followed me to the kitchen. He listened and agreed I needed better locks among other things. Then he left for a meeting with Nate. My mother had passed away eight years ago, so the meeting certainly was not related to a divorce. Nate and my father had been friends for years though, and Nate occasionally helped him out on legal matters. Maybe he was thinking about marrying his lady friend and was looking into a prenup.

It didn't matter as I was still reeling from the idea of Rick keeping watch all night. I couldn't decide if it was a good thing or creepy. Cleaning up the kitchen was my way of avoiding the issue.

My phone rang, yet another unknown number. It was Meredith and she wanted to talk. I agreed to meet her at Starbucks. As I drove there I decided I was going to have to make a run to Hunters Woods soon – I missed Dunkin' Donuts. For sure the pastries at Starbucks didn't compare. Once again, I ordered my coffee and waited.

"Hi, Stacie. Is it okay for me to call you Stacie?"

She came up behind me and she startled me. She was dressed like a model from a fashion magazine, a figure like a Barbie doll, and a bit overdressed for Starbucks. Her perfume wasn't overpowering, probably Chanel. I nodded and waited for her to continue, my Skinny Mocha in hand.

She scanned the lower level of the store and pointed to the stairs. It was much less crowded upstairs. She found a table for two in a corner.

I sat down and waited for her to speak. This was her show and it was only my curiosity that made me come. I didn't have to like it.

She took a sip of her latte. "Thank you for meeting with me. I know this is awkward and uncomfortable. If it helps, it's just as awkward for me. I won't apologize. Ted was very charismatic, successful, and brilliant. I was coming off a bad situation... We met when I got involved in Cornerstone."

She hesitated, waiting for that to sink in. "I needed an ego boost. I'm not sure what he needed. Maybe he needed to help someone. He didn't need me, at least not me personally."

She took another sip.

"I don't understand what you mean."

"He seemed more interested in my father than me. At first I thought the discussions on relational aggression and abusive spouses was related to my situation. But he knew my father was instrumental in getting a bill drafted specific to domestic violence and harassment. He somehow knew my father had worked with the NFL and other groups on domestic violence. It was all he ever talked about."

"One of his pet projects for sure, so I'm not surprised." Ted had read up on everything and worked behind the scenes to try to toughen the consequences for those involved in domestic violence. If he couldn't help Maureen, maybe he could help someone else.

"He asked so many questions though. I think he was onto something. You probably heard the rumor that I walked in on him with the domestic help?"

I nodded and she continued. "That was a story he contrived. After you found out… and he said you were naming me in the divorce. After he was sure others knew about me, or would know about me, he was afraid that our seeing each other would put me in danger."

"You weren't named. Only that he committed adultery."

"But mutual friends knew about me, knew my name. His father even bragged about it."

I winced. I could see him doing that. Finally, his son was with someone from the right niche in society.

"Sorry. I think it was because of his father he came up with the cleaning lady story. He both hated and loved his father and it was his way of sticking it to him. Hamilton was livid. Besides, then Ted wasn't worried about a nonexistent new cleaning lady being in danger. He let Mrs. Vittone go only a few weeks before he was killed. He'd used a service those last few weeks. He didn't even know the people who were cleaning his house."

"What was he afraid of?"

"I don't know. I don't know if it was related to Cornerstone or domestic violence even or something at the firm. The last few weeks he never relaxed. I think he was on to something or someone besides Mitch. I think that's what got him killed."

I stared at her. She drank her coffee and didn't say anything else.

"Have you told this to the police?"

"No. They called, but only asked about my whereabouts the night he was killed and our relationship. My father's lawyers were insistent I only answer the questions asked. My father was insistent I not talk about his interests or how we got involved. You know the drill I'm sure. Nothing that might cause a scandal is ever shared."

I shook my head. I didn't know what to say. She finished her coffee and stood up. "I'm sorry, Stacie. I hope you can use this information to help the police figure out who killed Ted."

She walked away and I sat there. Thoughts churned through my mind. Was there some connection to Cornerstone? Between Krumm and Mitch? Were some of those pictures of bruises perhaps not of Maureen, but of Meredith or someone else? A quick glance at my watch and I headed for a yoga break. Maybe something would come to me.

CHAPTER 16

When I got home, I called the police station and left a message for O'Hare. On a whim, I called Cornerstone. Shawna was busy and said she'd call me back when she got a break. A mother and two kids had arrived, traumatized physically and emotionally. I touched base with Jillian and she invited me to join them for Sunday dinner. Only after she promised Wade was cooking, did I agree.

Busying myself around the house, I looked at the second box again. Assuming the pictures were of Maureen and he already had them, O'Hare hadn't taken them with him. I decided to go through them again. I recognized a few of them as definitely Maureen. At least one of them showed the person's bruised hand and the ring on that hand wasn't Maureen's. It was way too small. I pulled any I couldn't identify as Maureen and set them aside.

The vacation files I planned to shred. Under the circumstances, I checked each piece of paper before shredding. I found a few more photos misfiled. One I recognized easily as Meredith with a black eye. Knowing that was what brought them together helped somehow. Likely Ted maintained contact in an effort to get her to press charges as he had with Maureen and their relationship grew from there. There was another log sheet like the other one as well.

I'd finished with the files when the phone rang.

"Hey Shawna. You finally able to take a breath?"

"You know weekends are the worst. The family and another solo since you were here yesterday. We're about at capacity."

I did the math in my head and asked, "Where did you put them all?"

Shawna exhaled loudly and I knew it wasn't good news. "The one on the rougher side you saw? She decided she didn't want to be here, she'd rather be back on the streets. Dr. Hanreddy asked a few too many questions I suspect. Probably a runaway. Scary to think that what she was running away from was worse than the beating she took on the streets."

"For sure. And the other woman?"

"She's doing better, though she's still not able or willing to talk. She's able to eat and drink now and stayed awake longer today. Sooner or later she'll have to make a decision as to where she goes from here."

"I know this is going to sound odd. I think Ted was trying to figure out something related to domestic violence or maybe somebody had an issue with Cornerstone. Any rumblings you know of?"

"You know Virginia has the community partnership group trying to identify and address the needs of sexual and domestic violence victims. They're doing trainings for responders and counselors with an emphasis on minority populations and poverty, given their reticence to report based on their experience with police. That is getting people riled up some."

"But that ignores the bigger issues for some with fear of what follows disclosure – the publicity, loss of status, bringing shame to the family. How often do the 'rich and famous' acknowledge these happenings in their own families? What about the power of money?"

I shook my head. How many times had we heard the "for the sake of appearances" line from Ted's father and sister?

Shawna and I commiserated on the problems and the reason places like Cornerstone existed, but not in an obvious way. I assured her I would be in the following Saturday.

I was about to call Veronica when my phone rang again. I now recognized the exchange as the same as the police department and answered.

"O'Hare here. I have a message you called."

"I did. Do you remember the pictures in those boxes? We thought they were the same ones of Maureen?"

"Yes, why?"

"I looked at them again and found a few more in the other file folders. They aren't all Maureen."

He mumbled something he probably didn't want me to understand. "Hold on to them please. I'll get them or have someone get them later." With that, he disconnected.

I stared at the phone and wondered if the call dropped. Somehow, I didn't think that was the problem. My next call was to Veronica to see how she was doing and how Andy felt, however my call went to voice mail. That left house cleaning and straightening up the mess in the study to keep me occupied. Maybe if I stared at that log, it would make more sense to me what it was and why Ted had it.

Later that afternoon, my father returned to the house. Laden with boxes, he marched into the house without a word. Nate followed behind him, shaking his head. Jasper jumped around wanting attention and Nate complied.

"Hi, Dad, Nate. What do you have there?"

"Where's your tool box, Stacie? We have work to do and a dinner to go to later on."

Confused, I turned to Nate. He simply shrugged.

"In the laundry. Can I get you coffee or something else to drink?"

"Coffee's good."

With that, my father set the boxes on the table and walked off in the direction of the laundry room.

"Stacie, your dad told me about the problem last night and the cop who was here? Everything okay?" He petted Jasper and got beat by a wagging tail in return.

"Someone broke in at Ted's and here. Then last night someone was here again. Nobody seems to know what he wants. Rick was concerned whoever it was last night would come back." It was my turn to shrug.

My dad came back with the toolbox he'd given me so many years ago. "Where's the coffee?"

I chuckled and went to get them each a cup. Then I watched as they quickly installed dead bolts in both doors and camera equipped motion detectors outside the front and back doors. Jasper chased after them at first, then took a seat and watched it all.

My father asked where my laptop was and installed a program. My screen now showed the area outside the back and front doors. Next he installed the same app on my phone.

"See here," he held out the phone so I could see its screen. "With this app, your computer and your phone will get a notification when there is any movement picked up by the cameras. Movement will also turn on the lights. Unfortunately, that will include any animals, so Jasper here will set it off when he goes out and comes in. And you'll set it off too. If you see a notification, you can click on it and it will show you who or what made the movement. And, Stacie, it's recorded."

Hmm. Reminded me of his warnings so long ago that he'd be watching when a date brought me home. Guess no kissing goodnight at the door for me.

Mission accomplished, the two old friends got ready to leave. As he walked out the door, Nate turned around.

"Stacie, are you still moving forward on changing your name back to Maroni? I have all the paperwork but haven't processed it yet. What do you want me do?"

"Process it, for sure. I think I signed everything already."

"I'll take care of it. Keep your eyes open for the notifications. Stay safe."

I hadn't done much and yet I was exhausted. All the locks in place, Jasper and I caught a nap and my phone alarm woke me up. I changed my clothes and drove to Jillian's for dinner. Wade answered the door and pulled me into a hug. He was the same height as Jillian and they were like two bookends – both fit and trim. One white and one black.

"Come on in. Potatoes and veggies are about done. Just need to throw the steak on the grill."

Jillian joined us in the front hall and gave me a hug. "You need to update us on Ted's murder. Are you still a suspect?"

"I guess that depends on whether I'm still the half-mil life insurance policy beneficiary."

Both of them stopped and stared, mouths and eyes reflecting their shock.

"Hey, it was a surprise to me, too. One thing's for sure, Ted was full of surprises. I'm sure he would have changed the policy by now, so don't go thinking you can help me spend all the money either."

Once they recovered, Wade continued cooking while Jillian and I got the table set.

"Stacie, who do you think killed him?" Wade asked as he served the steak, twice-baked potatoes, the grilled veggies, and a salad.

"I'm not sure. It's looking like it might be one of the junior partners, trying to eliminate his competition or stop Ted from exposing him of harassment. The man showed up at my house yesterday – pushed his way in. He was drunk and repugnant. I was just glad when Rick showed up with a box from Ted's."

"Rick, huh? Same guy from Creekview, right?" Jillian teased.

"Yeah. And later there was another problem. Veronica's husband interrupted someone trying to get in the back door. Rick watched the house all night."

Wade's eyebrows shot up. Working for one of the largest security firms in the area, he tended to be suspicious.

"Did you know he was there?"

"No. I called the police in the morning when I saw a strange car. The grouchy one, Flatt, showed up and identified the car as Rick's. Rick apologized for not telling me."

"And then what happened?"

"He came in and had a cup of coffee. Of course, when he went to leave, he ran into my dad."

I hadn't laughed when it happened but I laughed then. I only stopped laughing long enough to add, "And now, my dad installed cameras and motion detectors that will record movement. So everything will be recorded. If I ever do date again, no good night kisses."

Jillian's mouth dropped and she joined in the laughter. Wade stared at me a few minutes, then insisted I show him the program on my phone. The last recorded movement, thankfully, was me leaving. As we finished dinner, my phone beeped and Wade grabbed it.

"Stacie, were you expecting anyone? Is this that Rick again?"

I peered at the picture and then Wade. "No, that's Krumm. He said he'd be back."

Wade continued to watch Krumm until he walked out of sight.

"Nice system. What about an alarm system?"

"My dad's ahead of you. Someone is supposed to be by to install that tomorrow. Reston Security, I think."

"Good company. A lot will depend on you actually using it. Security systems are only so good you know."

I nodded and shared what O'Hare had said about the surveillance footage at River's Edge. We talked a little more about Ted and then Jillian shifted the conversation to me.

"So now you're a widow instead of a divorcee. What are your plans, Stacie?"

"Not much has changed. Nate is taking care of the paperwork so I'll soon be Stacie Maroni again. I like my job well enough. When I get the inheritance and the tax stuff is all straightened out, I may think about going back to school. Only I'm so much older than other students will be and I'm not sure I still want to get a degree in counseling. Maybe business or human resources. We'll see."

"What about socially? This Rick person seems to be around a lot and you liked him the night you met him at Creekview?

"He's nice, he's gorgeous. You met him. If I'd met him at Creekview and we went out, that might have been okay. Somehow Ted's murder is in the middle of it now. Awkward."

I shrugged and Wade tilted his head. "When it's all over – when they arrest the killer, will you be able to get past this, Stacie?"

"Maybe, maybe not. Who knows, I may have to drag Jillian and Trina to the Brick one of these days." We all laughed but I could tell Wade was not on board with that idea

CHAPTER 17

I'd missed a full week of work. I knew I'd have to deal with the "we're so sorry" routine sooner or later, and staying home was making me antsy. Besides, I dreaded a very full in-box. Rosie was the first one I saw when I walked in the building. Our own version of Rosemary Clooney in her older years, Rosie greeted me with a hug and marching orders.

"How are you holding up, Stacie? Your messages are stacking up and your mail? I hope for your sake some of it is junk you can toss."

"I'm doing okay, Rosie. My plan is to whittle down the messages and mail. Anything critical I should know about?"

As part of HR, there isn't usually anything more critical than someone leaving or being hired, the occasional promotion or raise. On the other hand, as the primary point person for employee assistance services, sometimes the calls were serious. I had no doubt Rosie had checked them all.

"You'll see on your desk. One person was referred to the emergency room. She was in bad shape. She hasn't been back to work, but her immediate supervisor has spoken with her. Lynisha is on it."

Lynisha and I were each other's back up. I'd have to follow up with her in case I needed to step in.

Hopefully, the ER staff had already taken care of referrals. I gave Rosie a hug and headed for my office. I could at least hide in there – maybe.

She hadn't been kidding about the stack of mail. Announcements of this trauma counseling training or that human resource conference had piled up. For now, they all just went into the trash. There'd be new ones next month.

Month end reports from last month could wait and went into a separate pile. A quick glance had me doing a double take though. The month end report on hires, fires, and reprimands was set up the same as the pages Ted had. I was distracted from that realization by the edge of something at the bottom of the pile.

I lifted the files and envelopes to get a better look and found a manila packing envelope. I didn't remember ordering anything and jumped back when I saw the return address. It was from Ted, postmarked the day he was killed.

I couldn't even touch the envelope. Knowing my last unknown caller had been the detective, I pushed the button to call that number.

"Detective O'Hare."

"Detective, this is Stacie Noth. Can you come to Foster's Insurance Group on Lafayette Avenue?"

"Mrs. Noth, how did you get this number? And why would I come there?"

"You called me from this number yesterday. I'm at work. There's an envelope in my office from Ted. That's why you should come here."

"On my way."

Foster's is located in the center part of Beckman Springs and although not a big city, this is where traffic tended to gravitate from all directions. With me driving, it would have taken about 20 minutes from the police station to my office. O'Hare must have used his lights and siren – he was there within 10 minutes. I heard his deep voice before Rosie arrived with him in tow.

"Thank you, Rosie. Detective O'Hare and I need to talk." I wondered if he had multiples of the same jacket.

She huffed but walked away. As I closed the door, I envisioned her with a glass or stethoscope on the other side of the door.

"Have a seat?"

"Thank you. The package?"

I pointed to it and he immediately donned gloves. He moved it gingerly and read the return address. "This Ted's handwriting?"

"It is. And his address and my office address, including the mail stop."

"Any idea when this arrived here?"

I shook my head. "This is my first day back at work since Ted was killed. The same day he mailed this. I hadn't gotten down that far but it stood out."

He put it down and pulled out his phone. I listened to him give directions and then he leaned back.

"We're going to wait for Flatt and Napoli. In the meantime, do you have a clear idea of how CO&N is organized? I know we discussed this before, but you know, who reports to who?"

"Sort of. The three partners each are over junior partners – Ted for one."

I thought back to the holiday parties and other events. "I'd guess there were about eight to ten junior partners at any time. The junior partners reported to one or more of the partners. Ted usually worked with Chameux and occasionally with Opinsky, never Noonan. Within the junior partners, some were more advanced. They worked on the more prestigious cases and were more likely to move up to partner as the firm grew or someone retired."

"So Ted and Krumm would be in that more advanced group?"

"Yes, and Ray Pierce I think. I'm not sure why he wouldn't be a consideration for partner, come to think of it. He's been there as long as Ted. Ted had a lot of respect for him."

"But not Krumm?" O'Hare countered.

"He never mentioned Krumm. In fact, I never met Krumm before he showed up at my house. He may have joined the firm in the past year and moved up quickly."

"What else?"

"Besides the partners and junior partners, a large pool of paralegals helped with research, discovery, and if they were good enough, even the initial draft of briefs. Ted had his favorites and being higher up on the junior ladder, usually got his choice. He called them his team. He would sometimes comment on Sally being the best for this new case he pulled or that he really needed Jacob's help on another one. Those were the two he talked about the most."

"What about the administrative assistants – like Veronica?"

"Those at the top of the junior ladder – the top three or four – each had their own admin. Most times, as a junior achieved some level of esteem with the partners, he was assigned his own admin to reflect the workload he took on. He could either request the admin from the pool or hire a new one. The others would share the admin pool. I don't understand why Krumm assumed Veronica would be his admin or what happened to his admin." I shrugged. "He must not have been that impressed with his own, but surely he realized Veronica was about to go on maternity leave?"

Voices coming closer ended our conversation. O'Hare opened the door for Flatt and Napoli.

"Rosie, could you grab an extra chair please?"

Eyes opened wide, she wheeled in a chair and looked around. "Anything else I can get for you? Coffee?"

We declined and she left. O'Hare made sure the door was closed, his hands still gloved. He picked up the packing envelope.

"Mrs. Noth found this waiting for her this morning. She has confirmed that the handwriting is that of her husband. As you can see, it has been sealed with packing tape. I am going to open it now. Scissors?"

I handed him the scissors and held my breath. He cut the bottom edge and allowed the contents to spill out onto the area of my desk I'd cleaned off.

"Now we know what he did with the external hard drive. We'll take this and figure out what to do with it. This is addressed to you."

O'Hare handed me a sealed envelope. My hands shook as I opened it.

> *Stacie, if you're reading this, it means I haven't been able to call you and explain why you received this package. You of all people know how careful I am about proprietary information and security. I'm mailing this to you at Foster's because this seemed the last place anyone would look for it. After some indications that someone tampered with the lock to my home office, I'm regretting not having better in-home security. Please don't say, "I told you so." My plan as I mailed this is to take care of that and then reclaim this packet. Please hold on to this and lock it away until I can figure out what to do with it. And Stace, don't tell anyone you have this. Thanks – You're still the best thing that ever happened to me. I'm sorry I messed it up and hurt you. Ted*

I handed it to him and reached for tissues. He put the hard drive and the letter back in the envelope after he read it. He glanced at the other papers. There were more logs.

"Any idea what these might be?"

Pulling out the monthly report for Foster's, I compared it to those sheets.

"This, here, is our monthly HR report. The ones in the envelope and the ones we've seen before have a similar layout – but without the headers and more extensive. I think Ted was looking at something related to HR. I don't know who does HR for CO&N or how often they look at turnover." I paused and O'Hare rolled his hand for me to continue.

"Here, I get reports monthly and have to compile the numbers with the information from exit interviews. I have to compile all the information to see if there is a specific area or section with more problems. For example, if one section has greater turnover than others from month to month, it may indicate a problem with the supervisor in that section. Definitely would need to check that out." I shrugged.

O'Hare gazed straight ahead and didn't say anything for a while. "Not sure what it means, but we'll take this back to the station and the Chief can sort out how to deal with it."

He finished putting the papers in the envelope with the external drive. "Stapler?"

I handed him the stapler and he stapled the end of the envelope across the bottom. They all signed on the stapled edge. He stuck it inside his jacket as he stood up. Flatt and Napoli stood as well.

"Please don't mention this to anyone." He patted his jacket. "We'll be in touch. Call if you find anything else."

He opened the door and had to catch Rosie. "I… I was just about to knock to see if you changed your mind about that coffee."

He shook his head and took a step out. He turned back at me with brows raised as Flatt and Napoli joined him in the hall. I stuck my head out the door and chuckled. The hall was lined with co-workers who on seeing the three men scampered back into their respective offices.

"Sorry, we don't get much excitement around here."

CHAPTER 18

I watched them leave and then went back to my desk. Before I had a chance to think about anything, Jillian was in my office.

"What was that all about? We heard the police were here to arrest you for Ted's murder. I think someone even called the media."

"Nothing of the sort. They just had some questions. That detective always has questions."

"You sure about that? This wasn't just the detective, but the two cops as well. It took three of them?"

I shrugged. "I don't think he likes asking questions without witnesses or a recorder. Maybe he's afraid of being accused of something."

"I hope that's all it is."

"Oh my gosh, Stacie, you need to pull up the news – right now." Trina stormed in like she was being chased.

"What?"

"The news. Someone called them. They're talking about you on the news!"

Within seconds I had the news on my screen and my phone was ringing. Caller ID warned me it was my father. I watched the news as I took the call and he confirmed that he was watching it at the same time. The headlines read "Police staged to make arrest in Noth murder" but the reporter on site told the story.

> *We received an anonymous tip earlier today that Beckman Springs police had a break in the murder of prominent attorney Theodore Noth and would be making an arrest here at Foster's Insurance Group. We had confirmation that the detective in charge, Detective O'Hare had arrived and asked to see Noth's estranged wife, Stacie Maroni Noth. Soon after two police officers entered the building. A few minutes ago, Detective O'Hare and the two officers exited the building. Detective O'Hare's response to the question regarding Mrs. Noth's pending arrest was a simple, "Does it look like I've arrested her or anyone else here today? This is an ongoing investigation and we will continue to investigate." When the officers were asked what they were here for, they simply responded, "Police business" and drove away. Obviously no arrest has been made. Watch for an update later today.*

"Stacie, what's going on? This is getting out of hand." From the tone of his voice, I could tell my father was frantic.

"I have no idea who called the media. I'm fine. They just had some questions, not even anything to do with me. The questions were all about Ted and CO&N. I'm fine. Please let everyone else know."

I disconnected and Jillian gave me a hug. She sat back down and Trina closed the door. "Okay, so now tell us what's going on."

"Like I said…"

My phone rang and noting the caller ID, I clicked. "Hi Nate. I'm fine, honest."

"Okay, but I have alerted Drew Paulson to be on standby just in case. I'm texting you his name and number."

"Thanks."

I sighed and looked at Jillian. "This is too much. I'm tempted to go home, but the media is probably still hanging around outside."

"Stacie, you're not going to get out of here right now. You might as well get some work done. We can order lunch in and figure out how to sneak you out later when everyone is tired of watching you." Jillian was the voice of reason, as always.

I nodded. "Okay, lunch at 12? You'll order and we can eat here?"

The rest of my morning was uneventful. Part of my job was to post the hiring notices for anyone seeking employment. I searched my email and found a handful. Once I checked to be sure all the required information was there, the position was posted into a portal.

One caught my eye in particular. It wasn't a posting after all, but a message from one of the Vice

Presidents that she would be seeking a replacement for her admin when her current one left for maternity leave in three months. The current admin had informally told her she would not be returning. No posting until that was in writing, but that would be a great fit for Veronica and good timing as well.

I continued to deal with files and folders the rest of the morning. No one came by and I wondered if it was because they believed I was a murderer. I hadn't figured out how to approach Rosie about who called the media or at least who she told who might have called the media. Of course, if she told two people and they each told two people, it could have been anyone. Close to lunch time, a knock on my open door got my attention.

"Hey, Lynisha. How's it going?"

"Good. You doing okay, Stacie? I know we're usually the ones helping others cope, but sometimes we need help too."

"Thanks. I get it. I'm hanging in, media aside. Right now I need to get a weeks' worth of correspondence sorted. And at some point, you'll need to fill me in on the crisis last week. But that'll wait."

"No problem. Maybe you should wait on crisis stuff for a while."

Part of me wanted to argue with her. I wasn't sure what she was thinking. Did she believe the media? On the other hand, I wasn't at my best.

"That's probably a good idea if you're willing to be primary for a while longer. I'm holding on, but barely."

She nodded and left. In a few minutes, Trina and Jillian showed up with our usual salads. We had a quiet lunch and Trina's patchouli was muted rather than overpowering. It wasn't my favorite of perfumes, but the musky scent suited her.

As they were ready to go back to work, Jillian stopped. "Stacie, I know you're swamped, but could I talk to you for a minute?"

Trina stopped as well and Jillian continued, "I'm having an issue with two of the people on a project and need some advice."

Trina shook her head. "I'm out of here then. Stacie, let me know if you need anything or want any company. Whatever, okay?"

I nodded and closed the door. Jillian stood at the door and started talking. "So anyway, there's this project and I have three people on it. Wait, let me get a bottle of water."

She opened the door and looked both ways. She whispered, "Grab your keys and bag. Let's go."

I wasn't sure what she was up to, but I followed her instructions. She held her hand up as we walked to the end of the hall and then signaled me to follow her. She checked her watch and picked up the pace as we crossed the back of the building. She stopped at the next exit.

"Wade should be right outside and he'll take you home. Let me know when you are safely away. Then call and let Rosie know you went home, still overcome with grief." She gave me a hug, opened the door and pushed me out.

Wade was there as expected. I hopped in his Jeep SUV and he drove away.

"Thanks, Wade. I'm not sure it was necessary, but thanks."

Then I saw trucks for all three media companies that covered the Reston-Beckman Springs area, along with a lot of cars and people. I instinctively ducked and we drove past undetected.

"Right now, it doesn't seem like the media know where you live. I drove by your house and didn't see anyone. Your phone beeping?"

"Only once. A cat."

"You have an unlisted number and address. In order to get your address from the Department of Motor Vehicles, they'd have to have a connection. With all the police you've made friends with down at the station, I don't see them handing out your information. This seemed the best way to get you away from the media."

"What about my car?"

"Eventually something big will happen – an accident, a robbery, a shooting, a politician spouting – and they'll decide you are old news. Then we can bring you back and get your car. And not worry about the media following you home."

CHAPTER 19

At home, I played with Jasper for a while and tried to regroup. The news crews were still in front of Foster's according to the local news website. The divorce was a nightmare, but this was worse. My father texted me the local home security group would be at the house at 4 o'clock. Then there would be alarms on the all the windows and the doors. I'd be safer than Fort Knox. Veronica called soon after I got home.

"Hi, Veronica."

"Call me Ronni, please. We're good. The doctor says 'any time' now. I only called because of the news. They are still out there. Are you alright?"

"Yes, Ronni, thanks. I don't know who called the media or who told them I was going to be arrested. They just had more questions. How is Andy?"

"He's good. Tell me, was anything in that box helpful?"

"You packed it, so you know what was in there. Any idea why Ted had HR reports?"

"I wondered as well. Maybe he was trying to find something to discredit Krumm. None of the admins who ever worked with him had a positive thing to say about him. I told you about the one who complained about him. She left shortly thereafter. I heard – now this is all rumor, you understand, and may not be true – that the turnover in paralegals has been pretty high, at least for the females, since Krumm was hired. Ted was upset after a meeting with Sally last month. She was one of his favorites and not for romance, believe me. She wasn't into men."

"Maybe he was looking for a pattern? Wouldn't HR do that?"

"HR at CO&N is limited as far as I know. They do the hiring paperwork and take care of benefits. I don't think they do anything except take care of transfers or cancellation of insurance and such when someone leaves. They haven't so much as followed up with me other than sending me all the paperwork for my family leave."

"So HR would know about Ted's insurance and any other policies?"

"Yes. The person you'd need to talk to about that is Becky Stallings. She handles all the life insurance, medical insurance, home insurance – you name it. She'd know if those policies in the box are the current ones in effect."

"Thanks. One other thing. The woman who complained, do you remember when that was?"

"It was about two months ago. What does that matter?"

"Ted's safe contained a log that covered 'something' from two and three months ago. I wondered if that coincided with her leaving. Veronica, do you by any chance know what kind of car Krumm drives?"

"A flashy red sports car. I know why you're asking that. Ever since the detective came to visit, I've tried to remember if anyone at CO&N drove an Escalade. Even after seeing pictures of Escalades, I couldn't remember one in the parking lot. Ever. Now that doesn't mean no one has one. It could be they have one but it's not the one they drive to work."

"Have you given any more thought to what you're going to do?"

"My leave officially started when I was in the hospital. I have accrued sick leave so I'm getting paid for at least the next month and then I can use vacation time. So far I haven't figured out next steps after that. After all that's gone on, Andy isn't too keen on my going back to CO&N. Neither am I."

"That sounds reasonable. Please keep in touch and let me know when Elle arrives, okay?" I decided not to mention the possible position at Foster's yet.

"You bet and you take care of yourself."

After we disconnected, I collected the insurance policies and called CO&N. I asked to speak with Becky Stallings. When the transfer went through, I started what I hoped should be a simple, straightforward conversation.

"Hello, Ms. Stallings, this is Stacie Noth, Ted's wife."

"Umm, umm. Yes, Mrs. Noth?

"The police delivered some insurance policies to me the other day. One of them is on me and I'd like to verify Ted had that one cancelled. Can you do that?"

I heard someone in the background and a click.

"Yes, ma'am. If you have the numbers, I can tell you if Mr. Noth cancelled it."

I rattled off the numbers of the two policies. Obviously, at least one should have been cancelled. And waited. I heard muffled sounds and realized she'd put the call on speaker. Maybe calling the insurance company directly would be better.

"Ma'am?"

"Yes, Ms. Stallings."

"We have a cancellation on the John Hancock one. We have no record of the other one."

"Okay. Can you tell me if you have a record of a change in beneficiary on Ted's New York Life policy? I don't need to know who it is, I just want to verify it is not me."

I heard a lot more mumbling before Ms. Stallings responded.

"Mrs. Noth, I think you need to call them directly for that information."

"Thank you for your time."

I hung up and cuddled Jasper for reassurance. At least calling the other two companies, I'd be more likely to get someone who hadn't seen the news this morning. It took three transfers before I was able to engage someone at New York Life. As I expected, I was no longer listed as the beneficiary on the New York Life policy. I'd let O'Hare know so he could find out who was getting that half-million.

Next I tackled Globe. Same run around. Surprisingly, the policy on me was still in force. I advised them of Ted's death. Pending verification, they would transfer the policy to me for payment and change in beneficiary. Nice to know my life was insured though I wasn't looking forward to seeing the monthly payment.

I sat on the sofa and pondered the turmoil my life had become. Jasper joined me and gave me kisses. He'd been there that night. If only dogs could talk, he could tell me who killed Ted. I was beginning to realize that even if I wasn't a suspect – and the half-million life insurance policy no longer gave me motive – the craziness wasn't going to end until the killer was revealed.

I was still pondering this when my phone beeped to tell me there was a person in my front yard. Glancing out the window, I spotted the Reston Security van in the driveway. I saw part of one person and then another person approaching the door. The doorbell rang, and I could see the uniform through the peephole in the door. I picked up Jasper and opened the door to find a man and a woman. The man appeared to be older than me and obviously ate well. He was the one to speak.

"Ma'am. My name is Trevor Peacock and one thing you need to know up front. No security system is going to work if you don't ask questions or request ID before you open the door."

I blinked and looked to the woman.

"He's right. I'm Kelly Springer. We're here from Reston Security to install your security system."

I stepped back to let them in and didn't bother to explain I had seen them on camera. I probably still should have asked for ID. "Come on in. My father texted me you were coming."

They nodded. "Can you walk us through and we'll figure out what we need to bring in? Will it be easiest for you to have the alarm controls by the front or the back door?"

"Front. Come on let me show you around."

"Nice dog. What's his name?" Kelly moved closer and Jasper licked her hand. One thing about Jasper, he was a friendly dog.

"Jasper."

"He's sweet but not exactly a watch dog, huh?"

I gave Jasper a hug in case he realized she'd just insulted him. Then we walked through the house. They counted windows, got their equipment, and before I knew it they were through. They had me enter and re-enter the code I chose to arm and disarm the alarm.

They reminded me to be sure my phone was always with me as any breach would send a message to my phone. If I didn't answer within two minutes that all was safe, the police would be notified. They repeated this multiple times along with the charge that would be incurred if I was home and didn't cancel the alarm.

CHAPTER 20

By the time they left and made sure I turned the alarm on, I already hated the thing. But for the time being, it would be worth the peace of mind for my father and for me. Although they had cleaned up some, residue from their work was everywhere – on the windowsills, the floor, and counters. Time to clean up.

As I vacuumed, I realized that Jasper was sleeping in the new bed and hadn't gone near his old bed. I decided to vacuum out Jasper's old bed and maybe even wash it. Probably not at the top of Ted's to-do list. Weird, a scrap of material was under the cushion with what looked like a blood stain. Jasper had never bitten anyone to the best of my knowledge.

I put it aside, not sure what to make of it. Jasper spotted it and bared his teeth. He growled and hissed. When I picked him up, he snapped and then seemed to calm down when he couldn't see the scrap any more. Once again I thought to myself, if only dogs could talk.

I put him outside and the alarm text came and the beep for someone in the back yard. I realized I had opened the back door with the alarm on. I sent the safe message and disarmed the alarm system. I'd have to remember to reset it after I let him back in.

Then I examined the scrap of fabric closer. It was silky soft, a pastel pattern with butterflies. Definitely from a female based on the scent. I didn't recognize the fabric or the scent, but both seemed expensive. Maybe Meredith's? The new housekeeper? The edges were tattered as if ripped off the main piece of cloth. Could Jasper have bitten the person who came into the house that night? I carefully stuck the scrap in a plastic bag and then in a drawer so Jasper couldn't see it or smell it. Then I called the Police Station and left a message for O'Hare.

The doorbell rang a few minutes later. I glanced at the laptop picture and saw a Beckman Springs police car. Just to play it safe, and avoid getting yelled at again, I peered through the peephole before I answered the door. It was Rick.

"Hi. O'Hare said you left a message about something you found?"

"Yeah. Come on in."

"Sorry about the run in with your father. Did that all get smoothed over?"

I chuckled. "Yes, and he and Nate have done their best to be sure I'm safe." I pointed to the alarm box and the dead bolts.

"Disarmed? What's that noise?" He looked past me as he spoke.

"Oh, that's Jasper." I walked into the kitchen, talking as I went. "He got all upset over the piece of material and I had to put him outside."

I opened the door and Jasper immediately went to Rick, tail wagging.

"What material? Is that what O'Hare was talking about?"

"Yes. I found this scrap of material in Jasper's bed from Ted's house. I think it has blood on it."

"And you just noticed this today?"

I glared at him and his tone. "I only just noticed that instead of sleeping in his old bed, he was going to the new one. I was vacuuming it and then going to wash it. That's when I found it."

"Are you going to let me see it?"

"Jasper has to go outside first. He went a little crazy before. Besides I got the impression you weren't supposed to be on this case." If he could be hostile so could I.

He looked away and then took Jasper outside. He came back in and put his hands up. "I'm sorry if that came out wrong. You're right. O'Hare didn't want me to be anywhere near you or this case. He's given up on that. I still can't tell you anything but neither of us can seem to avoid my being around. Sorry, if that's a problem."

"No, it's not a problem, Rick. I just got the sense O'Hare had an issue. That's all. You seemed like a nice guy at Creekview and you still seem like a nice guy."

An awkward silence followed, which I broke by pulling the baggie out of the drawer.

"This was in the dog bed. That looks like blood to me, but I don't remember Jasper ever biting anyone. And when I pulled this out and he saw it, he went crazy. That's all I know."

Rick took the baggie and studied it for a minute. "I think you're right about the blood. It may not be anything but I'll bring it in to O'Hare. Too bad no one noticed when it was at the house, though."

He took the baggie and I followed him to the door. "Be careful. The killer's still out there and someone thinks you have something. This might be what the person was looking for."

He left and I let Jasper back in, locked and bolted the door, and re-armed the alarm. I could tell this was going to get old fast.

I was starting to get hungry and was about to call Jillian when the app sounded to let me know someone was in my front yard. It was Wade's Jeep SUV. I disarmed the alarm and met Jillian and Wade at the door.

"Hey Stacie. We came by to get you for dinner and then get your car from Foster's. Now everyone has left, the media has given up. Thankfully, no one except Trina and I know where you live or they'd probably be camped out here."

"My neighbors would sure love that. Come in and let me show you how safe I am now." I showed them the app on my phone with them walking up the driveway. I explained about the alarm system and armed it as we left.

We ate at Luigi's and once again my phone beeped with Krumm in the picture. He left but it was still creepy.

"I know I should feel safe with all this 'stuff' but somehow a person out there would be better."

"Maybe Rick will watch the house again. Or is he through stalking?"

"Stalking? I don't think so. And we had words today. He's only hanging around because he can't avoid it. Besides he saw all the alarms. He only stayed that one night before deadbolts, cameras, and alarms."

Jillian could tell I was miffed about something and changed the subject.

"Every one at Foster's was talking about you the rest of the day, you know. This is the most excitement ever."

"What were they saying? They don't really believe I'm a murderer, do they?"

"Most don't. In fact, most couldn't figure out why you'd kill Ted. Then there were some who said he deserved it."

"Geesh. Nobody but you, Trina and Lynisha came by after the media circus. I checked and I barely even got an email."

After much discussion, I decided that I'd let Rosie know in the morning that I needed a few more days off to cope with Ted's death. I only hoped by then the killer would be found. In the meantime, I'd work from home doing what I could. And get in some yoga, maybe help out at Pet Connections.

CHAPTER 21

Decision made, the relief of not having to face my co-workers and boss the next day had me in good spirits. As I drove home, I sang along with *Journey*. Changing lanes, I noticed a black car behind me. I took the turn and it was still there. And I was sure it was an Escalade. Feeling paranoid, I reminded myself it was only paranoia if someone wasn't really after me. I told the phone to call Beckman Springs police.

"Is this an emergency?"

"I think so. This is Stacie Noth. My husband's murder is an open investigation and a black Escalade may have tried to run me down last week. I think one is following me right now. Detective O'Hare is the detective on the case."

"Your location, ma'am?"

I gave her the cross street I'd just passed, turned and gave her the next cross street.

"Okay, ma'am. I'll relay the message to Detective O'Hare and officers in the area. In the meantime, if you turn left at the next intersection and then right you should be at the Police Station in about 15 minutes."

"I'll do that. Then what?"

"When you get here, call back and someone will come outside to you."

"Thank you."

I reached the first intersection, turned and made the next right turn. The car was still behind me. At least we were in traffic and not on some isolated road. I drove the speed limit and turned up the music as a distraction. My phone rang as I stopped for the light about seven blocks before the police station. Unknown caller.

"Hello? Who is this?"

"It's Rick. O'Hare's tied up. Car still behind you?"

"Yup! I'm still about 5 minutes from the station. At the light at Alexandria."

"I'm at the next cross street and will try to pull in behind the Escalade. You need to pull into the station and wait. Got it?"

"Got it."

The light changed and my music came back on when the call disconnected. The car was still behind me. I reached the police station and pulled in. Whoever was in the Escalade must have realized the error of their ways. They immediately sped away with one cruiser right behind and two more joining in the chase. I turned off the car and waited.

A knock on my window startled me and I jumped. It was O'Hare.

"Come on inside and we can fill out the report while we wait."

I followed him in and back to the same nondescript room. He asked about everything that had happened since he'd left Foster's. I filled him in, highlighting my sneaking out of Foster's and the new alarms and cameras, while downplaying the interaction with Rick. And then noticing the car behind me as I left Foster's to go home.

"Any particular reason you noticed it? Was the person following too closely or driving sporadically?"

"Nothing that obvious, no. We had just discussed that if anyone knew where I lived the media would be camped out at my house. I kept checking to see if I spotted a media van or anyone following me from Foster's that could be media. I wasn't expecting to see the Escalade."

"Could you read the front license plate? Even part of it?"

"No, I couldn't see it clearly for some reason. Did you ever check to see who at CO&N has an Escalade?"

"Yes, we checked, but only for the employees. No one. If a spouse or other relative owned one, we still wouldn't know. Or they could rent or lease. There are a lot of Escalades in Beckman Springs and the surrounding area. No way to figure out which one might have been trying to hit you."

His phone beeped and he scurried out with "Be right back." A few minutes later, he returned shaking his head.

"Whoever was driving is crazy. He drove into the wrong lane and caused accidents as people swerved to avoid hitting him. The officers chasing him had to stop and give aid. He got away."

"I hope no one was hurt."

"I don't know for sure. Hopefully, someone got a good look at the front license plate. The back one was covered." He shook his head again.

"Okay, Stacie. Who knows your new address?"

"Jillian and Wade, Trina, and Nate. Hamilton Noth. My father. Obviously Krumm. And Andy. My insurance agent. Any company that bills me for anything. And anyone who noticed the address on the divorce papers or on the bulletin board in Ted's kitchen."

"Okay, so Krumm must have gotten the address as a result of being in Ted's house?"

I nodded.

"So he had to have been in Ted's house. He said he was looking for notes, so he may be the person who searched both your houses. Who else would have been in Ted's house?"

"Mr. Noth was there when I put the note on the bulletin board. I don't know if his mother or sister or Mitch ever visited in the last six months. Usually the family functions were at Mr. Noth's home, not ours. Meredith? If she was at the house, and I know she was, she would have seen the note. Mrs. Vittone? Whoever Ted hired when he fired Mrs. Vittone."

"He hired a group called 'We Clean Houses' – mostly college age girls who need a little extra money. They confirmed they had the code to get into the house and the guard logged them in and out. And we checked, the codes to the house, the gate, and Ted's office were all different."

"That's odd. The house and the gate used to be the same. I never tried the office. To make them all different? He was being careful."

He nodded.

"Did you ever find the gun? Or check to see who had a gun? Was it Ted's?"

"No, it wasn't Ted's, or at least he didn't have a gun permit. The gun hasn't surfaced. The assumption is the person brought it with them and still has it or ditched it some place. Based on ballistics, it is most likely a small handgun, probably a 9 mm. The kind most often bought for concealed carry."

I shrugged. "I don't know anything about guns. Never wanted to know anything about guns." I hesitated but then asked, "Do you think it's possible that Jasper bit the killer and tore that piece of fabric off in the process?"

"No idea. It's been sent to the lab and they'll let us know if it's blood and if there's enough for blood typing or DNA. It could be Jasper snagged the piece because it had blood on it and not because he caused the blood. I didn't see anything that resembled teeth marks. It also could be totally unrelated to Noth's murder."

His phone beeped and he stood up. "Can I get you something? Coffee, water?"

"Water would be great. Thanks."

O'Hare came back in and shook his head. "There were several injuries. Thankfully, no fatalities. Unfortunately the front plate was covered as well. We'll contact all the body shops and Cadillac dealers to let us know if an Escalade comes in with a dented passenger door. Probably a few other scrapes and dents as well."

"Your officers okay?" I really only cared about one of them.

O'Hare's mouth twitched. "They're all fine. Probably will be hung up for a while directing traffic and getting all the cars sorted out."

He stood up and I followed suit.

"Anything else?"

"Remember that first log you found at Ted's? I think he had those in relation to an admin who filed a complaint against Krumm for harassment. She wasn't taken seriously and she quit. That would have shown up on the logs from that time period."

"You know this how?"

"I remembered Veronica mentioning something about an incident and asked her about the time line. It matches."

"It could be a coincidence, you know. Any way to connect that to his written notes?"

"I think he may have been tracking who left and who they worked for last. For that one, the only person she worked for was Krumm – that could be the one that he circled." I shrugged. "Obviously, that's just a guess."

He nodded. "Might be a possibility."

I drove home cautiously, and despite O'Hare's reassurances, I took a few extra turns. I dashed into the house, disarmed and immediately re-armed the alarm system. Jasper jumping at my feet and spinning around clued me in I needed to disarm it again.

It was dark out and I waited to disarm until after I let Jasper out and the lights came on. As soon as he came in, I re-armed it. I fed him and filled his water bowl. For myself, I fixed a bowl of Rocky Road and drizzled chocolate syrup on top.

As I was about to sit down and enjoy it, my phone beeped and I saw Krumm walking up the drive way as the motion detectors added more light. The doorbell rang and Jasper started barking and growling. To add to the cacophony, Krumm started pounding on the door and spewing profanity.

I waited to see if he would stop, but he didn't. I called the police to report it and the dispatcher advised me the police were already on their way. Sure enough, my phone beeped as cruisers pulled up to the house and Krumm stumbled around. I watched him fight with the police until they had him safely secured in one of the cruisers. Finally, Jasper stopped barking.

Shaking his head, O'Hare walked toward the door and knocked. I disarmed the alarm and shouted "Who is it?" so I wouldn't get yelled at. O'Hare responded and I let him in.

"At least this time you checked. Nice alarm system." He checked it out and nodded.

"Thanks. What was Krumm's story?"

"Not sure. But he'll be sleeping it off at our expense tonight. We'll see what tomorrow brings. Stacie, your neighbor's call came in before yours. Why'd you hesitate?"

I shrugged my shoulders. "It seems like calling 9-1-1 is becoming too habitual. I was hoping he would give up and go away."

"Until we get Ted's killer, it should be habit. You need to call as soon as something feels off. You get it?"

Hanging my head, I nodded. "Okay, I'll keep that in mind."

He turned and left. I re-armed the alarm and curled up with Jasper. I didn't care that my ice cream was almost melted. I ate it anyway. Someone to share the sofa and the movie with would be nice.

CHAPTER 22

The next morning, O'Hare called and said he would be coming to the house to update me on the investigation. Both nervous and excited at the prospect of this nightmare ending, I made coffee and neatened up just to have something to do. Jasper kept tilting his head at me as I bounced around the house. When O'Hare arrived, I was surprised Flatt and Napoli weren't with him.

Disarming the alarm, I opened the door and let him in. "Coffee? It's fresh."

"No, thanks. As I said, I wanted to bring you up to date."

I nodded and waited.

"First off, Krumm arranged to be released on the drunk and disorderly early this morning."

"So he's likely to show up here yet again, huh?" I sighed. So much for my wishful thinking.

"I don't know about that. I'm pretty sure the District Attorney has what Krumm was looking for. It was on the external drive. You were right. Ted had compiled documentation across the 13 months that Krumm worked at CO&N. Specifically, the paralegals who either requested not to work for him or resigned. Those who left had been assigned to Krumm more than once and were female. The second time they quit. Including Sally most recently. Ted had checked and in most cases they had worked for Pierce or him previously, as well as for some of the other more junior partners, some with very positive reviews from others."

He paused before he continued. "The same pattern emerged with the administrative assistants, Krumm had fired one admin, one had requested to be re-assigned back to more junior partners, and two had resigned. Ted had documented and confirmed a clear pattern of sexual harassment and a hostile work environment. He shared the information with Chameux the week he was killed."

"That explains why even with Ted dead, Krumm wasn't a shoe-in for partner. How did Krumm even know Ted had the evidence?"

"Chameux admitted that he talked to Krumm after Ted showed him what he'd found. Krumm tried to say it was all fake news and Chameux said they had no choice but to investigate the situation."

"What happens now?"

"The evidence was turned over to the District Attorney and he issued a warrant. Krumm barely got home and was arrested for sexual harassment, sexual assault, and possible rape based on what Ted had on the external drive. CO&N has been notified and consideration is being given to issuing warrants for those the women complained to as complicit in taking no action despite the repeated documentation provided to them regarding sexual harassment. The District Attorney wonders how many others will come forward from previous positions when the charges are made public."

"Did he kill Ted?"

O'Hare exhaled and shook his head. "No, he didn't. Krumm admitted to searching both houses for the notes and the report Ted created. He had an alibi for the murder – a high-priced call girl who wasn't likely to forget him and his aggressiveness. He doesn't own an Escalade. He claims he would never own any car so common as a Cadillac. Amazingly, he also doesn't have a permit for a gun."

"Where does that leave us?"

"We'll keep looking, but you still need to stay safe." With that, he stood and left. I re-armed the alarm system and drank my coffee. I'd see if I could address any of the issues in my work email or private email.

I played with Jasper and was getting restless when my phone rang.

"Hello?"

"Hi Stacie, this is Ronni. I wanted to call and let you know baby Elle arrived yesterday."

"Oh, that's so exciting! Congratulations! How big was she? How are you both doing?"

"She was 7 lbs, 6 oz and 20 inches long. We are both doing well – no complications at all. I'll probably be going home later today."

"That's great. Has your mom arrived yet?"

"Andy's gone to pick her up at the airport. What about you? Any news?"

I filled her in on Krumm's arrests and she was glad to hear something had come from Ted's diligence in addressing the harassment.

"But he didn't kill Ted?"

"Nope. On another note… Please let me know when you're ready to go back to work. I think there may be an opening coming up for an admin at Foster's Insurance Group."

"I'll do that. And when we get past the first few weeks, you'll have to come meet baby Elle."

We disconnected and I hugged Jasper. Looking for the silver lining from this nightmare, I now had a new friend. Bored, I decided it was time to go visit Pet Connections and walk some dogs.

CHAPTER 23

It had been a quiet few days. In fact, I hadn't heard from O'Hare in at least 24 hours. We'd gone over all the other possibilities I could come up with and were back to some of the same questions. If not Krumm, then who? He also let me know that the half-million was to create a foundation that would fund services and research related to victim services and domestic violence. Senator Langford and several others would be heading up the Theodore Noth Foundation.

Mitch was the only other person Ted in any way threatened. But O'Hare said Mitch had an alibi for the night Ted was killed. He was at a real estate conference in Vegas and several people confirmed seeing him that night. Talking about Mitch, it occurred to me I hadn't talked to Maureen since the funeral. Feeling guilty, I decided to give her a call.

"Hi, Maureen. How are you holding up?"

"I'm okay. It's been hard. I can't believe Mitch is gone."

I stared at the phone, surprised at her comment. "I'm sorry Maureen, I don't understand."

"Oh, I assumed you knew and were calling to gloat. Ted and you finally got what you wanted. Mitch had no choice but to leave. That nasty detective made that clear. He as much as threatened to leak those photos to the press if Mitch didn't leave. So Mitch left quietly and moved to the New York office."

"I see." I didn't really and her tone was angry and directed at Ted and me, not Mitch. "So, you'll be getting a divorce?"

"Of course not. A divorce would be a scandal. I'd never be able to show my face at the country club. I would be a nobody like you. You never understood all that was at stake. At least you have an excuse, being working class. Ted knew what was at stake and he kept pushing me anyway. He should have minded his own business."

"I'm sorry." I disconnected, my feelings very conflicted. Ted worked so hard to fight harassment and abuse, fueled by what he saw happening with Maureen, and still she didn't get it. Instead, somehow Ted became the bad guy. Disconcerting to say the least.

About an hour later, relaxing on the sofa with Jasper after cleaning the kitchen, I was surprised when my phone beeped and caller ID showed Maureen's name. She said hello and got straight to the point.

"I realized I wasn't very nice when we spoke earlier. I'm still in shock you know. Ted's gone, Mitch is in New York, the house is very empty."

"I'm so sorry, Maureen. That is a lot to handle, but it will get better." My thumb accidentally hit speaker.

"I'm not so sure…" As Maureen's voice came out of the speaker, Jasper growled and hissed. I clicked speaker off and stared at Jasper.

"What was that?"

"Jasper. Something must have bothered him. You were saying?"

"That dog is vicious. I never understood why Ted got a dog from a shelter instead of a purebred from a breeder. Anyway, I called to see if you would join me for lunch at the country club today."

In all the years Ted and I had been married, she'd never invited me to lunch. Odd. Maybe she was lonely and wanted to talk about Ted.

"Well, I… I guess I could do that."

"Thank you. We can meet there and talk about Ted. That would be a great help."

Still odd, but if it would help her move on. Maybe I'd be able to convince her to get some counseling. I could couch it under grief counseling for Ted's death and then Mitch's move.

I pulled out a dress I hadn't worn since the last time I went to an event at the country club. It was a lot less loose fitting to be sure, but not too tight. With any luck, no one would remember it six months later. I didn't really care if they did.

I arrived on time and waited in my car to make an appearance an appropriate ten minutes late. At the desk, I didn't recognize the woman who greeted me.

"I'm here for lunch with Maureen Dantzig. Has she arrived yet?"

The woman looked at her chart. "I'm sorry. I don't see that she has a reservation. Are you sure you were to meet her here?"

"Yes, ma'am. I'll give her a call and see if something has come up."

Stepping outside, O'Hare called as I pulled out my phone.

"Can you come in to the station? I have some information and some questions."

"I'm at the country club right now to have lunch with Maureen. I can come by after lunch. Here she is now. I'll see you then." For a change, I disconnected on him.

"I'm so sorry to be late, Stacie. Shall we go in?" Her dress was black with a colorful sash. Very fashionable with Jimmy Choo slingbacks. Her crocodile purse matched her shoes, but seemed too big for the dress. I'd have expected a small clutch with that dress.

"After you."

I followed her in and the woman who'd been rude to me beamed at Maureen. "Mrs. Dantzig, how nice to see you today. Can I help you with anything?"

"Yes, Dorothy, I need a table for two for Stacie and me. Do you know Stacie? She was Ted's wife."

Not understanding why she added that, I smiled as Dorothy glanced my way. She worked magic on her computer and said, "Right this way, please." Odd, she didn't respond to Ted's death. Forgotten already.

We followed Dorothy down the steps to the dining room. Not much had changed since my last visit. All the tables were adorned with fresh flowers that would be replaced with candles for the dinner hour, and of course, fancier linens.

Dorothy seated us by a window that overlooked the golf course. A beautiful view, though I wasn't a golfer so I only appreciated the aesthetics.

Our waitress came and poured our waters. "Anything else to drink today, ladies? I believe we still have mimosas available at the bar."

"Oh, I'll have a mimosa, my dear. What about you, Stacie?"

"Too early in the day for me. Do you have the strawberry lemonade today? That was a favorite of mine."

"I'll get those for you while you decide on your meals."

The menu hadn't changed much and I decided to go all out and get the salmon. This would be on Maureen's bill as there was no exchange of cash at the country club. She ordered a salad. I chastised myself that was probably why she was still a size 4 and I wasn't but decided I deserved the salmon for the tension.

"Thank you so much for joining me for lunch. I'm sure you've missed your visits here. They have a new chef and he is fantastic."

I sipped my lemonade, while I racked my brain to remember what events would be going on. "Glad to hear it. Isn't there a charity golf event coming up?"

"That was last week. I understand they raised a lot of money for scholarships. Didn't you get a scholarship for college?"

"Yes, I did. Scholarships are very important for a lot of young men and women. Did you participate in the tournament?" Somewhere in the back of my mind I recalled that Maureen and Mitch sometimes golfed as a twosome.

"Not this time." Her smile waned and I realized that by last week Mitch had already moved to New York.

"How are your mother and father doing? Have your grandparents gone back to California?"

She huffed. "Yes, they've returned. I'm scheduled to go visit them next month. They belong to the Mariota Country Club. I'm sure you've heard of it. Many actors and politicians are members. There will be a fundraiser for Senator Howard Rush. Senator Langford and Meredith will be attending as well."

I nodded while experiencing the familiar sensation of having someone subtly stick needles in me to remind me of my place in society. "That sounds wonderful. I'm sure you'll enjoy it. Besides, a change of scenery will be good."

Her demeanor shifted for microseconds with hostility showing before she regained the smile. Thankfully, the waitress arrived with our food. As I ate, I wondered again at her motive for this luncheon. Any thoughts I had of encouraging her to see counseling vanished.

"So how is your salmon, Stacie? I wish I had your bravery to eat what I wanted and not worry when I gained weight.

"It's delicious. As you said, the chef is wonderful." I smiled and ignored her jab.

Conversation waned as we ate and I added a roll to my plate despite her raised eyebrows. At this rate, if eating meant I didn't have to talk, I might finish the whole basket of them.

"Stacie, I always wondered, it's obviously no longer relevant, but why didn't you and Ted have children?"

"I'm sorry. As you said, it's not relevant now."

"I guess I was wondering if Ted had frozen – you know – in case there came a time…"

A light dawned and I wondered if Mr. Noth put her up to this lunch to find out if it were possible for me to give him an heir.

"No, Maureen. When we decided to get married, Ted and I agreed that we didn't want to have children of our own. I was already in my 30s and he was absorbed in trying to make partner. We discussed the possibility of adopting a child or maybe two after he made partner."

"Why not have children after he made partner? Ted was conceived when father was hired at the firm. I was conceived when he made partner. Yes, he was older by then…"

I shrugged. Ted and I had discussed possible issues with my fertility and his fear of spawning more sons like his father many times. Deep down, I don't think he wanted his father to have a grandson he could make miserable. And having a granddaughter was not an option.

"And then we would all have a piece of Ted left. Are you sure he didn't...?"

"I am. Lunch was good, but I have errands to run. And I probably shouldn't eat dessert." In the back of my mind, I realized Ted did a lot of things I didn't know about, so it was possible. He'd had a vasectomy so I wouldn't have to take birth control pills and there would be no chance I'd get pregnant, but he could have.... I certainly wasn't going to share this possibility with her or her father. I glanced at my watch. This had been a quick lunch.

"Let me sign the check and we can walk out together."

CHAPTER 24

While we waited on the server, I looked around the dining room. I recognized a few from the funeral. As I scanned the room I noticed a woman who resembled the one from Cornerstone – the one in bad shape. She shook her head slightly and then turned away talking with her friends, a smile plastered on her face. It made me sick to think how many of the "rich and famous" were maltreated, emotionally or physically, and thought this was a reasonable price to pay. For what?

"You shook your head, Stacie. Is there a problem?"

Gathering my composure, I smiled. "Not at all. Just thinking of all I need to do."

The server came and Maureen signed with a smile. As we exited, she made it a point to tell Dorothy how good the food was and how much I enjoyed it.

"This was a great idea, Maureen. As always, if there's anything I can do to help…"

"There is one thing before you leave. I have something in my car I need to show you."

I shrugged. "Sure. Something to do with Ted?" She nodded and I followed her, thinking I was getting yet another copy of our wedding picture.

The parking lot for the country club was U-shaped and I had parked toward the back but in the front of the building. I followed Maureen as she walked around to the side.

"Maureen, why'd you park way over here? There's plenty of spaces right in front."

"I prefer to park here sometimes. Not as easily seen."

True, for sure. Though I couldn't fathom why she wouldn't want to be seen at the country club. We passed the few other cars, likely employees' cars. The only car left was a black Escalade. A black Escalade with a large dent in the passenger side.

"You know, I just remembered I have to be somewhere. Whatever it is you need to give me? I can get it another time."

I turned to sprint but she grabbed my arm. Then she pointed a small handgun at me.

"No, you see that won't do. You see, that detective won't leave me alone. He forced Mitch to move away, but he keeps coming back. And he always has more questions. I decided the best plan would be for you to kill yourself after confessing to killing Ted. You can be appropriately remorseful, sorry for putting people through all this."

My mouth dropped and I was speechless. All I kept thinking was that I could not get into that car.

"We just had lunch and I'll tell them how distraught you've been. Guilt was just too much for you. That detective is getting pressure to close this case. He even came to see me today right after you called."

"What did he want this morning?"

"I'm not sure. He asked about our cars and he asked if I'd ever been to the house Ted and you shared. Silly to call it yours when my father owns it. He asked if I knew where you lived now. Nothing really. He just keeps asking questions."

"Why did you kill him? Your brother?"

"He had a big fight with my father at dinner that night. First about someone he worked with and then about Mitch. He threatened to take both stories to the media. He taunted our father with his relationship with Meredith and his connections to the Senator and how involved the Senator was in stopping domestic violence."

I nodded. I didn't know what to say and I only hoped an employee came out to leave and saw her with the gun.

"Without Mitch, I'm nobody. He has the money and the power, and without him or someone like him I wouldn't be accepted. It's bad enough that I haven't been able to get pregnant. Mitch and father talked about in vitro fertilization or possibly using a surrogate. If Ted went public with his suspicions, my world would be destroyed. Divorce is not an option. Mitch is in New York due to growing pains and business concerns, you understand."

I nodded again. I glanced past her to the car, wondering what her next step would be.

"I have a pad of paper in my car. You'll write out your confession while I drive to the creek. Then you'll kill yourself. I'll tell them you pulled the gun and forced me to drive you there. Of course, I was afraid you would kill me, too, but instead you killed yourself. When you and Ted become old news, Mitch will come home and life will resume like normal."

"You do know being beaten up by your husband isn't 'normal' right?"

She waved the gun and I took a step back. "You don't understand. Now get in the car!"

"No, I won't. You can kill me right here. You're planning on killing me anyway. In fact, I may just walk away. You'll have a hard time with your suicide story if you shoot me."

"You don't think I'll do it, do you?" Then she aimed and I felt a sting in my upper arm. But no noise; no one would have heard the shot. I gaped at my arm and the blood dripping down.

As I glanced back to her, I thought I saw something move between the cars. Once and then again. The cavalry perhaps.

"I said get in the car."

My legs wouldn't move. My mouth wouldn't move. I surveyed the parking lot to see where someone might be now.

"What are you looking at? I said get in the car."

"A cat. I saw a cat or something between the cars."

She moved just slightly and I took a step away. At the same time, a deep voice I recognized as O'Hare's bellowed, "Mrs. Dantzig, put the gun down on the ground. We don't want to hurt you."

She turned and grabbed at me, then aimed the gun at me. Then I fainted. Again.

"Stacie, Stacie. Are you okay?"

Opening my eyes, I glanced up at the sky. Then I noticed the two men by my side. Rick and someone else in green scrubs.

"Ma'am. We're taking you to the hospital to have your arm taken care of. Before we start this IV, is there anything you're allergic to? Do you hurt any where else?"

I shook my head and turned to Rick. "What happened?"

"It's over. Maureen is in the other ambulance and under arrest. Don't worry about that now. Let these guys take care of you. I'll stop by later to check on you. Oh, and Stacie, when you get a chance, you better call your dad – you're on the news again."

He squeezed my hand and watched as they loaded me into the ambulance.

CHAPTER 25

As soon as I could, I called my dad, Nate, and Jillian. The shot had grazed my arm and the doctor was in and out cleaning it, then leaving the nurse to bandage it. She'd finished and now I waited on the doctor to release me. Jillian had volunteered to pick me up.

"Mrs. Noth? How are you feeling now?" Dr. Higgins did something with the IV, disconnected it, and then removed it. She checked the bandage and waited.

"As well as can be expected after being shot. I'm not in pain if that's what you're asking."

She smiled. "Sounds about right. We gave you a topical anesthetic and a mild pain medication through the IV so I'd be surprised if you were in pain right now. Is someone coming to pick you up?"

"Yes. She should get here soon."

"Good. You shouldn't be driving. You can take over the counter pain medicines like ibuprofen for any discomfort. With ibuprofen, you can take up to 800 mg, but best to take it with food so you don't upset your stomach. Call if that isn't sufficient."

"Anything else?"

"Try not to get it wet for the next 24 hours."

I nodded but cringed. How was I supposed to take a shower?

Dr. Higgins smiled. "I'm afraid you may have a scar as a reminder. We'll see. Your paperwork is all done. Here are your discharge instructions, including your next appointment for a re-check, and a list of symptoms that may mean I need to see you sooner. The nurse will wheel you out when your ride gets here."

Jillian, Wade and I rehashed the past two weeks once they got me home. I'd no sooner shared that Rick said he would stop by after his shift to check on me, and my phone beeped and showed him on the front step. Wade did the honors of inviting him in.

Rick was in jeans and a t-shirt, not on duty. I hoped that meant his visit was more personal than official. He had a bag in his hand.

"Hi. I guess you met Wade, and you know Jillian. Have a seat. Would you like something to drink?"

"This is for you. How's the arm?" He sat down and Jasper jumped onto his lap.

As he handed me the package, I caught his woodsy scent. The package was cold. I opened it and smiled. A half-gallon of Rocky Road ice cream. Everyone else laughed. Blame it on the medication, I got weepy that he remembered.

"Thank you."

Wade took the bag from me and tapped Rick's arm. "I'll put this in the freezer. I'm getting myself a beer. You want one? Or coffee or water?"

"Water's good. Thanks, man."

Rick looked back at me and gestured to my arm. I realized I hadn't answered him.

"Arm is still numb but tingly. I think the anesthetic is starting to wear off. I'm not quite as loopy as I was."

Jillian laughed. "We had a slight problem with the alarms – she couldn't remember the code at first and they had to disarm it remotely. Your detective intervened to take care of that."

"We've been talking it all through. Can you add any information?"

He nodded and waited for Wade to get settled.

"It was interesting to say the least to watch O'Hare interview her. She didn't want to call a lawyer, not even her father. She smiled at O'Hare and told him she was sure he'd understand this was all a mistake and let her go when she explained it all to him. Of course, he recorded everything and was very clear about her Miranda rights."

He shook his head. "I've seen O'Hare conduct interviews and I've never seen him interrupt to ask again about an attorney or repeat the Miranda warning. At one point, he decided he had to stop the interview, but I'll share the gist of her story."

We all looked at each other and waited for him to take a sip of water.

"She explained that Ted continued to push Mitch's treatment of her, which she still refused to acknowledge was battering or abuse. She characterized it as stress and alcohol getting the best of a good man. He was always sorry afterwards, promised it wouldn't happen again. When Ted wasn't getting anywhere with his father, he tried to talk to his mother and that was more painful. Mrs. Noth tried to explain Mitch's behavior as a woman's lot in life. He got in a big fight with his father and accused him of abusing his mother. Maureen heard the argument and although both parents denied any physical abuse, she knew it was only a matter of time before Ted ruined her life."

"We'd considered that, about his mother. He didn't believe it, but wondered if his mother had suffered similarly and he'd just never noticed. He couldn't accept that as a possibility though. I never saw any evidence. Perhaps it was years ago."

Rick continued, "That was the night he was killed. She went to the house and he let her in. She explained how he gave her a pep talk, told her he'd help her leave Mitch. She asked for all the pictures she'd heard him brag about having. Even then she had a bruise on her neck and a scarf on to try to hide it. She'd cut herself earlier and gotten some blood on the scarf. Ted tried to find out where the blood came from. She said he was screaming and waving the scarf and Jasper grabbed hold, tearing off a piece of it."

"Okay, so that's how the piece of fabric ended up in his bed."

Jillian and Wade exchanged glances and their faces reflected confusion. I explained about finding the piece of the scarf and giving it to the police. Then we all turned back to Rick.

"Then she pulled a gun on him and Jasper started barking and growling. She told him to put the dog outside or she'd shoot him. Jasper was put in the back yard where he was found the next day. With the gun in hand she told him she wanted the pictures – then he'd have no proof. Ted let her in to the office and tried to talk to her. He refused to give up the pictures and she said she had no choice but to kill him. Jasper was barking and howling so she left."

"So she confessed?"

"Yes, but O'Hare was concerned she would recant and say she only said it under duress. Still is. That's when he stopped the questioning, asked her again about an attorney, and she made a comment like 'You understand, right. I had no choice.' O'Hare called her father and let her sit there for a while."

"Then what happened?"

"Noth came down and O'Hare let him in the room with her. Noth glared at Maureen and berated O'Hare for interrogating her without an attorney present. Noth accused O'Hare of harassment and anything else he could think of. O'Hare hit the rewind to about halfway and pressed play. Noth turned several shades of red as he heard O'Hare prompt her every time she took a breath about an attorney."

"He must have been furious with her."

"I don't know about Noth's relationship with his wife, but he made to smack Maureen and O'Hare restrained him."

Silence followed this statement.

"So it was her blood on the scrap of material?"

"Not sure. Insufficient but the blood on the fabric scrap was definitely from someone related to Ted. That's why O'Hare stopped at the Noth and the Dantzig homes this morning."

"But she didn't mention the scarf when she was talking about his questions."

"He asked general questions, however he did notice the Escalade with a dent. That's why he called you and why when you said where you were and with her, he managed to get people in place. Unfortunately, not quickly enough to avoid you getting injured."

Jillian followed the conversation and asked, "Wait. If she didn't trash the houses, who did and what were they trying to find?"

"Krumm was the one who broke in. First at Ted's, and then here. He was searching for all those HR reports Ted was going to use to confront the partners and put a stop to the sexual harassment. Apparently Ted was particularly upset when one of his paralegals was ready to quit. He pulled rank to get her permanently assigned to him."

"Sally."

Rick nodded and stood up. Jasper barked once and looked up at him, not happy to give up the lap.

"You know, you guys laughed at Jasper as a guard dog, but he only growled at two people – Krumm and Maureen. If I'd paid attention when he reacted to Maureen's voice, I never would've gone to lunch."

Every one laughed and Jasper jumped up on the sofa with me.

"It's been a long day and I'm sure you want to get some rest. There is one thing though." Rick winked as he spoke.

"What?"

He turned to Wade and Jillian and then to me. "Could one of you come with me to get Stacie's car from the country club. The station got a request to ticket and tow. Everyone is a little too busy right now to get to it." He winked again and Wade left with him.

Jillian helped me get changed and by the time Wade came back I was definitely ready for sleep. They said their goodbyes and as they were leaving, Wade turned back.

"Rick and I had a nice chat on the way to get your car, Stacie. Plan on going to Creekview Lounge again some time when this is behind you. Jillian and I will drive you and maybe Trina can come too. What do you think?"

"What? Really? When? What will I wear?"

"Whatever it is, I'm sure everything will match!

CHAPTER 26

It had been a month since Maureen's arrest and I felt human again. I'd been to see Ronni, Andy, and Elle. They'd seen the news of course. As the District Attorney predicted, the number of additional complaints against Krumm had risen. Ronni's name was now on that list. Ronni shared that HR at CO&N was still under scrutiny and certainly would not ignore a complaint in the future.

Both O'Hare and Rick stopped by to check on me that first week. Not surprising, Mr. Noth had managed to get Maureen into a private psychiatric facility. Her attorney said she was incapable of participating in a defense or understanding the proceedings; her psychiatrist agreed. From what Rick and O'Hare related, the wrong of what she did escaped her. The means for her justified the end – her position in high society.

I still couldn't resolve how she ended up this way. It couldn't be only a function of her home life or that she was battered. Ted grew up in the same family, albeit as a male, and he died because he cared about her and other women like her. All of this made me very glad to be your basic middle class HR representative and slowly but surely losing the "Noth" off the end of my name.

All the mysteries aside, I was a nervous wreck when Jillian told me we were going to the Creekview Lounge. Not sure I even wanted a do-over of my night out at Creekview, I hoped Rick would be there. I wasn't sure if I wanted to see O'Hare either. Jillian told me Wade called the police station and let both of them know we'd be at Creekview.

I dressed in a lightweight, cobalt blue sweater, jeans, and boots. My hair fell in loose curls and appeared to be natural – after many attempts to get it that way. I put on makeup and spritzed my favorite Banana Republic Rosewood perfume.

"Do I look okay, Jasper?"

He barked and wagged his tail. Then my phone beeped. Too late now. Jillian, Wade, and Trina had arrived. Wade was to be the designated driver and try to keep all of us ladies out of trouble.

Trina talked and laughed, very animated during the short drive to Creekview Lounge, punctuated by Wade rolling his eyes. It was still pretty early, only a few of the booths were taken. Wade ushered us to the bar. "Better view and easier for anyone to spot us."

With that in mind, we staked out the end of the bar. With the three of us, someone might think Wade had a harem. Hopefully, no one decided that because he was black, he was a pimp and we were his hookers. Trina's outfit, as usual was a little risqué, the streaks in her hair now purple to match her top and fit that assumption.

The bartender, Halsey by his name tag, wasn't very friendly so I wasn't too sure what he thought of our group. He glanced over at us with a frown, and no friendly greeting.

"Halsey, could we get some drinks here please?" Jillian asked.

He sauntered over, but not too close and directed his question to Wade. "What will you have?"

"Me? I'm the designated driver tonight. Fresca or Coke, please. The ladies are on their own, though I will pick up the first round." We all ordered and Wade paid promptly, declining the invitation to run a tab.

The DJ put on Dio's Stand Up and Shout! and Trina shrieked. "We have to dance! Come on." She dragged Jillian and me out to the empty dance floor. It wasn't long before a man came up and started dancing with her and others joined us on the floor. Jillian and I beat it back to the bar before anyone else got any ideas.

Trina stayed on the dance floor song after song. I faced the bar. Jillian stood next to Wade, his arm around her. They scanned the crowd and kept watch on the door, checking as people came in. I itched to turn around. Instead I sipped on my wine and joked with Jillian. Then Wade whispered, "Incoming."

Unable to help myself, I turned around as Rick and some others reached us. He extended his hand. "Care to dance?"

"Sure." I smiled and we danced. He was a good lead and the woodsy scent was nice.

Before we joined the others, he offered with a gleam in his eye, "Hi. I'm Rick Murdock."

I chuckled. "Nice to meet you Rick. I'm Stacie Maroni."

His left brow went up.

"Officially changed on my driver's license as of today." I didn't add what a weight that was off of me.

He smiled and guided me back to the others. Trina and her new friend, Bill, had joined the group as well as O'Hare. O'Hare was deep in conversation with Wade about his security firm and some issues in the next town. Ended up that Bill also was with the Beckman Springs Department. Napoli, who quickly became Marina, looked more feminine in skinny jeans and a tunic top than she had in uniform. Her loose curls added to the picture. She engaged Halsey a few seats away and our service improved.

Rick handed me a glass of Viognier and sipped on his scotch and soda. We danced and chatted with our friends. As we were all ready to leave, he leaned over and kissed me. This time I didn't cry.

ABOUT THE AUTHOR

Welcome to Beckman Springs, VA – no, you won't find it on any map. *Prestige, Privilege and Murder* is the first in a new mystery series, mostly cozy in its lack of graphic detail and the requisite amateur sleuth. Stacie Maroni is an HR specialist, counselor, and dog lover. As this is Stacie's debut novel, I'd love to hear what you think. It will be fun to see what kind of trouble she and her friends can get into as she moves on with her life after Ted's murder. You can expect to see more of Jillian, Wade, Trina, and Ronni, and of course, Rick. Hopefully, Stacie's interactions with the Noth family will be a thing of the past.

I love mysteries – reading and writing them. I previously published the *Cold Creek Series*. The main character in the Cold Creek Series is a professor turned amateur sleuth. I also teamed up with Cassidy Salem to develop the teen/young adult *Hannah and Tamar Mystery* series. Although the characters are teens, these novella-length mysteries also may appeal to the young at heart.

You can see all my books on my Amazon author page http://www.amazon.com/-/e/B00G8SBCKK or

Goodreads
https://www.goodreads.com/author/show/7257539.Christa_Nardi

I'd love to hear from you - you can find me:
Facebook: https://www.facebook.com/christa.nardi.5
Twitter: @ChristaN7777
Email cccnardi@gmail.com
Blog: Christa Reads and Writes (christanardi.blogspot.com) where I mostly post reviews of others' books with an occasional update on my writing.

You can subscribe to my newsletter at http://smarturl.it/ChristaUpdates - I send out only one newsletter per month with information on sales, works in process, and upcoming new releases.

Special thanks to my great beta readers!

Made in the USA
Columbia, SC
14 May 2018